THE ENCYCLOPEDIA OF
Brazilian
JIU JITSU

VOLUME 2

(Revised Edition)

RIGAN MACHADO AND **JOSE M. FRAGUAS**

EMPIRE BOOKS
LOS ANGELES, CALIFORNIA

Published in 2020 by Empire Books/AWP LLC.
Copyright © 2004 by Jose M. Fraguas & Rigan Machado. All rights reserved.

Library of Congress Cataloging-in-Publication Data
NAMES: Machado, Rigan; Fraguas, Jose M., authors.
TITLE: Encyclopedia of Brazilian Jiu Jitsu / by Jose M. Fraguas & Rigan Machado.
DESCRIPTION: Los Angeles, California: Empire Books, 2020. | Description based on print version record and CIP data provided by publisher; resource not viewed.
IDENTIFIERS: ISBN: 9781949753202 | 9781949753219 | 9781949753226 (pbk.: alk. paper)

1. Jiu jitsu-Brazil-Encyclopedia I. Fraguas, Jose M. II. Title GV1114.M339 2020
796.815 '2' 0899103-dc22

2994002550

EMPIRE BOOKS/AWP
Los Angeles, CA 90049

First Revised Edition

20 19 18 17 16 15 14 13 12 11 10

PRINTED IN THE UNITED STATES OF AMERICA.

"Nothing determines who we will
become so much as those things
we choose to ignore."

—Sandor Minab

Dedication

To the memory of Carlos Gracie, the first member of the Gracie family who trained in the art of Jiu-Jitsu.

To Professor Helio Gracie, a true pioneer who broke barriers and put himself to test on behalf of his beloved art. His study and sacrifice paved the road for all future generations.

Acknowledgements

The creation of the *Encyclopedia of Brazilian Jiu-Jitsu* has been very much a team effort since the authors conceived this book in 2001.

Special thanks to the members of the Machado and Gracie family, whose permission to quote and peruse from personal notes has given this text its core.

To Doug Jeffrey, editor of the work, for his time and effort cleaning and polishing the manuscript. Your help and dedication are truly appreciated.

To Todd Hester, editor of *Grappling* magazine, for his encouragement and expert advice for this work.

To Carlos Gracie Jr., president of the Brazilian Confederation of Jiu-Jitsu from Rio de Janeiro, Brazil, for his priceless support and cooperation throughout the project.

Additional thanks are extended to Kid Peligro, a columnist of *Grappling* and *Gracie* magazines and dedicated Brazilian Jiu-Jitsu practitioner, who allowed the authors to use some photos from his personal archives.

To Jaimee Itagaki, photographer at CFW Enterprises, who put in many hours behind the camera capturing all the technical details.

To all the students who provided excellent cooperation and skills while demonstrating the techniques that you see on these pages.

Finally, we want to thank all the students and practitioners around the world whose support and dedication to the art has tremendously helped to promote and popularize the art of Brazilian Jiu-Jitsu.

adidas

Table of Contents

About the Authors

RIGAN MACHADO

Rigan Machado, whose lineage is linked directly to the art's founder, Carlos Gracie, is one of the top Brazilian Jiu-Jitsu instructors in the world. His long experience in teaching — to everyone from beginners to world champions — and his contributions to the art's teaching methods have brought him worldwide acclaim. Originally from Rio de Janeiro, Brazil, Machado's personal credits include many of the top Brazilian national and international championships. Furthermore, Rigan Machado was one of the first Brazilian black belts who moved from Brazil to the United States of America, where he became one of the leading forces in expanding the art. *"Brazil was just the beginning of the grappling movement,"* says Machado. *"From there, the seeds have been spread all around the world. If a student is not from Brazil and he becomes a world champion, then that makes me a good teacher and makes me happy."*

Despite his fame, he continues to train with a dedication born out of the love of his art. Machado has also appeared in several movies and television shows, becoming one of the most recognizable figures in the world of the martial arts. Highly regarded as one of the most talented technicians and teachers who ever came out of the Gracie family, Rigan has been instrumental in the development of Machado Jiu-Jitsu as it is known today.

"Finding a harmony between mind and body is the ultimate goal of any martial artist, but the physical techniques must come first," he says. *"A calm and concentrated awareness is the key toward the realization of personal potential, of which the technical mastery is the first step."*

Drawing from his considerable knowledge, Rigan Machado has written extensively on his art and authored several series of DVDs on Brazilian Jiu-Jitsu.

JOSE M. FRAGUAS

Born on October 25, 1962, Jose M. Fraguas had his first contact with the martial arts (the grappling art of Judo) at the age of nine. Practicing as a child under Sensei Young Lee in Madrid, Spain, Fraguas progressed rapidly until he decided to pursue a different but related martial art style. The seeds of contact sports, however, had been planted.

Recognized as an international authority on the martial arts and author of many books on the subject, he began his career as a writer at age 16 by serving as a regular contributor to martial arts magazines in Great Britain, France, Spain, Italy, Germany, Portugal, Holland and Australia. Having hands-on experience and training allowed him to better reflect the physical side of the martial arts in his writing. He started his training in Brazilian Jiu-Jitsu in the late 1980s with several members of the Gracie family.

"I would love to mention the members of the Gracie family who spent so many hours in private and group classes sharing their knowledge with me, but I am afraid that crediting them with being responsible for my Jiu-Jitsu skills would make them feel more pain than pride," Fraguas says laughing.

His desire to promote both ancient philosophy and modern thinking provided the motivation for writing this book. *"I want to write books so I can learn as well as share."* Fraguas continues, *"The martial arts are like life itself. Both are filled with experiences that seem quite ordinary at the time and assume a fabled stature only with the passage of the years. I hope this work will be appreciated by future practitioners of the art of Brazilian Jiu-Jitsu."*

Jose Fraguas currently lives in Los Angeles, California.

History

PART 2

THE GRACIE CONNECTION

The art of Brazilian Jiu-Jitsu started when Mitsuyo Maeda (Count Koma) decided to rebel against Japanese tradition and taught Gastão Gracie's oldest son, Carlos, in return for the diplomatic support Gastão gave him in establishing a Japanese immigration colony in the north of Brazil. Carlos was so fascinated with the techniques he learned from Maeda that when the family moved to Rio de Janeiro in 1925 he opened the first Gracie Jiu-Jitsu Academy. During these early years, Carlos made a great effort to teach different law enforcement groups and police departments the effective techniques Count Koma had shared with him. Carlos, a very intelligent man, dedicated most of his time during the first years in Rio de Janeiro to promiting and publicizing the art and teaching in the academy.

Helio, his younger brother, was physically very frail and doctors prohibited him from participating in any kind of physical exercise that could make his health worse. In fact, Helio was ordered to avoid any kind of physical exercise at all. During the classes that Carlos taught at the academy, all Helio could do was sit on the side and watch the students practice. For several years, that was all Helio was allowed to do inside the walls of the Gracie Academy. For Carlos, the health of his brother was far more important than teaching him the ancient fighting techniques of samurai Jiu-Jitsu.

"During the classes that Carlos taught at the academy, all Helio could do was sit on the side and watch the students practice."

But the history of the art was changed forever when Carlos couldn't make it to the academy one day for one of his private classes. The student showed up for class and Carlos wasn't there. Helio, only 16 years old, offered to teach the student himself, so the client wouldn't lose a day's practice. Helio told the student that he knew the moves because he had watched his brother teach them every day for the last two years. The student accepted the offer and Helio Gracie taught the first class of his life.

Later, Carlos arrived at the academy and tried to apologize to the student for his tardiness. But the student replied, "Don't worry; your brother Helio taught me. If you don't mind, I would like to take classes with him from now on." Carlos was shocked but also extremely proud of his younger brother. With the blessing of Carlos, Helio became more active in the teaching duties of the academy. Soon, he found himself teaching

the vast majority of the students. Carlos, an excellent nutritionist, focused more and more on the development of what is now known as the "Gracie Diet." A phrase by Hippocrates, to "make your food your medicine," was the trigger for Carlos to dedicate his life to the nutritional aspects so important to the Gracie family training methods. He also allocated time to managing the fighting careers of his younger brothers. With Carlos busy researching nutrition and managing the family's business aspects, young Helio's role in the academy increased. In the art of Jiu-Jitsu, he found the love of his life. But all was not perfect.

"Instead of relying on strength and explosiveness, Helio began to use leverage and body mechanics to achieve the same results."

While the techniques taught by Maeda to Carlos were extremely effective and useful, they didn't fit Helio exactly. With a small frame and weight of less than 140 pounds, Helio soon found out that many of Maeda's techniques weren't suitable for his slight physical structure. He began a process of analyzing the techniques taught to his brother and modifying them to allow him to use them against bigger and heavier opponents. Instead of relying on strength and explosiveness, Helio began to use leverage and body mechanics to achieve the same results. Subtle changes in the techniques allowed him to devise an arsenal of moves that could be used with much less strength. Out of necessity, Helio Gracie devised a unique fighting system based on proper positioning instead of physical force. Under the guidance of his brother Carlos, Helio started to fight. Although Carlos was worried about his brother's health, Helio surprised everyone but himself when he beat all the opponents he fought. In only 30 seconds, via armlock, 17-year-old Helio beat professional boxer Antonio Portugal and laid the cornerstone in the construction of the Gracie Family dynasty. Fighters such as world wrestling champion Wladek Zybskus and Japanese Jiu-Jitsu champion Nakimi were soon on the receiving end of Helio's revolutionary fighting methods and masterful technical skill.

Not only did Helio Gracie create a name for himself and his family, but also for generations of Gracie fighters to come. His fame reached as far as the "Land of the Rising Sun," and so Japan sent the lightweight Judo champion, Kato, to face the Brazilian hero. It was time for a Japanese master to stop that "rebel," they said. Little did they know that Helio was going to defeat Kato via a chokehold at the Ibirapuera Arena in Sao Paulo, after the first fight between them was declared a draw. A commotion in Japan occurred and the open weight champion, Masahiko Kimura, was sent to regain the honor taken from the Kodokan. On October 13, 1951, the greatest soccer stadium in the world, Maracana, was packed to watch the fight between the Brazilian

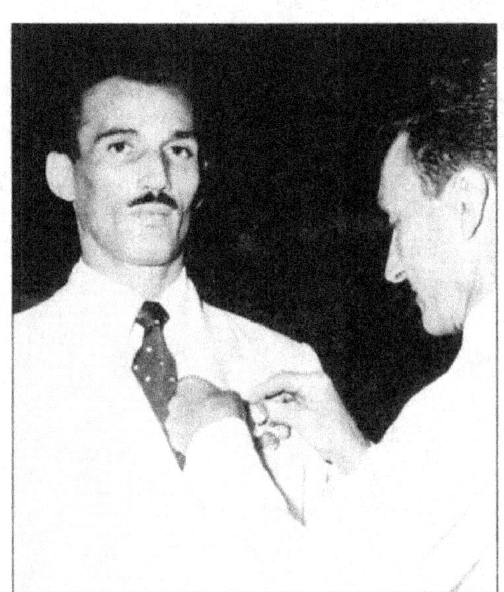

national hero, Helio Gracie, and the Japanese champion Kimura, who is now widely regarded as the greatest Judo fighter of all time. Helio was 42 at that time and weighed 140 pounds. Kimura, in his prime, was 34 and weighed 195 pounds.

Kimura, very confident in his abilities and his superior strength and size, said that if Helio lasted more than three minutes without being defeated, he should consider himself the winner. Helio fought Kimura for a little more than 15 minutes, and brother Carlos threw in the towel only when Kimura got Helio in a painful armlock. Helio didn't seem to be willing to tap at all, so Carlos decided to stop the fight before any major damage could be done. Impressed with Helio's performance, the Japanese masters invited him to Japan to teach the modified version of Jiu-Jitsu that he had developed. Helio, understanding the difficulties of leaving his family and his academy to go to a foreign country, graciously acknowledged the compliment but declined the offer.

The many legendary fights of Helio Gracie include the longest fight in history when he faced Waldemar Santana on May 24, 1955, for 3 hours and 45 minutes in a non-stop fight. Searching for fame, Santana, who was Helio's student, had

made disrespectful comments about the Gracie family. Helio answered by coming out of retirement and challenging him to fight. Although Helio lost the fight, his courageous performance won him the hearts of the Brazilian people. During his fighting career, Helio also issued challenges to some of the greatest boxers in history such as Primo Carnera and Ezzard Charles, but the most notable was when the great Joe Louis declined to fight against the Brazilian master.

During his entire life, Helio Gracie has proven to be a courageous and determined individual. With the support of his older brother, Carlos, he created one of the most efficient styles of self-defense known to man, and he left his own blood in the ring to perfect it. Carlos became very spiritual in his later years and tried to reach higher of level of consciousness by dedicating more time to meditation and perfection of the Gracie Diet. Both brothers made a tremendous contribution to future generations of martial artists all around the world. Carlos died at age 94, filled with the peace he sought, while quietly taking a bath. Helio Gracie is recognized as the father of the Jiu-Jitsu style he developed, which is now known around the world as "Gracie Jiu-Jitsu" in his honor.

"Carlos became very spiritual in his later years and tried to reach a higher level of consciousness by dedicating more time to meditation and perfection of the Gracie Diet."

Introduction

IMPROVING YOUR GAME

Finding the proper way to improve your game is one of the most difficult things to do. After years of training, every Jiu-Jitsu practitioner reaches a point described as "hitting the wall." It is here when more training won't necessarily bring the desired results. More is not better anymore. The choice of your training partner is paramount here since your improvement will be based not on your partner's general skill but in his ability to bring the best out of you.

At this point, your partner becomes your "training coach." Try to put yourself in a worst-case scenario and work from there. For instance, if your guard is your weak point, dedicate the beginning of your personal training to work other aspects of the game. When you are tired, ask your partner to try to pass your guard. This is a difficult situation for you due to two factors: 1) you are already exhausted and, 2) you are going to work on the weakest part of your game.

"Have your partner feed you with several approaches. Ask him to not use brute force but technique and deception. If your partner doesn't follow what you are asking him to do, replace him."

You must always try to stay calm. This specific training should be highly technical. Ask your partner to attack your guard using a flowing approach. Don't let the egos come into play here. "Play" is the key. Have your partner feed you with several approaches. Ask him to not use brute force but technique and deception. If your partner doesn't follow what you are asking him to do, replace him. This is your way of improving and if he doesn't cooperate, choose someone who does.

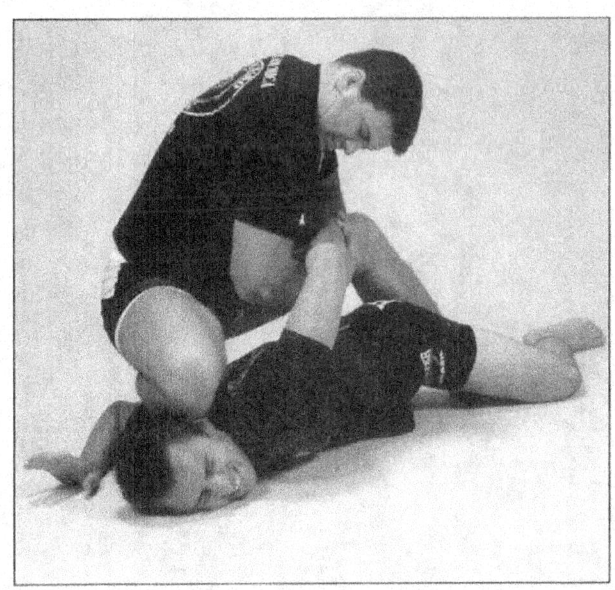

MAKE IT FUNCTIONAL

The road to excellence is long in any sport, and Brazilian Jiu-Jitsu is no exception. From the very first moment when a practitioner learns a technique until he applies it successfully in a world championship, there are many hours of hard training and progressive technical development.

There are four phases to achieving mastery of any physical technique: *to learn, practice, master* and finally *functionalize* it. We'll analyze each one separately and explain how the different concepts apply to each one of these training phases.

"The mind should navigate the body. Don't rush and try to use force because all the data that you'll be putting into your body will be incorrect."

1) Learn: This is the very first step. The instructor teaches the student the movement (technique) and gives him all the necessary technical details to perform the technique correctly. He walks with the student through all the basic elements and principles that build the foundation of that particular movement. The student now has all the information about how to perform the technique correctly, but he still lacks the training. This is the reason he doesn't perform it well and has difficulty executing it. It is important to be neither aggressive nor to use a combative mind in this phase. It is paramount to empty and relax the mind, trying to absorb as much as information as possible about the fine details of the movement.

2) Practice: Now that the student has the basic information, the next step is to practice what he already has (in his mind). This phase is extremely important since all the fundamental body mechanics for that specific technique will be built during this phase, which means that he must pay very close attention to how he inputs the information into his system. Taking time while absorbing and working on the little technical details of the movement is very important. The mind should navigate the body. Don't rush and try to use force because all the data that you'll be putting into your body will be incorrect. Relax and work slowly, little by little, paying full attention to each small detail that the teacher corrects.

Progressively, and only when the student has a fair amount of control on the "little details," should he start to increase the speed used to perform the movement. If he feels like he is having problems in achieving any "segment" or "section" or if the movement is less than correct, then he should slow down the pace and work on that particular aspect of the technique until it is fully corrected. Paying complete attention to each small detail is extremely important in this phase of training.

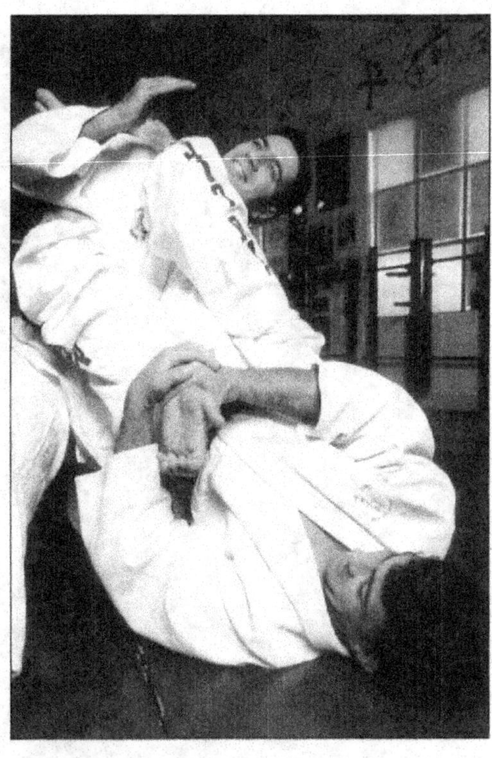

3) Master: This is a tricky word that brings confusion to the practitioner. He already has a very good level of skill in performing the technique as a "mold," but now he needs to add a new element into the equation... different opponents who give him different scenarios. Here, the practitioner doesn't need to think about the small details of the physical movement anymore — because these should be already in the database — but he needs to be able of fit the technical movement into the structure of different, uncooperative opponents. Uncooperative is the key word, because no two opponents in the world have the same way of moving, giving the same exact energy back or trying to counter the technique.

This first aspect of mastering the technique has to do with the operativeness of the technique in itself and your ability to understand how the technique should be used against different kinds of opponents. You should research and go deep into the essential principles of the technique and its possibilities under different kinds of circumstances (opponents). When facing a problem, don't try to find the solution outside the fundamental principles of the technique but analyze this new situation and try to find a way using the essence of the principles that compose the basic movement.

Don't randomly change the technique for the sake of change, but make the technique fit into the new scenario as you maintain

"You should research and go deep into the essential principles of the technique and its possibilities under different kinds of circumstances."

the basic principles of it. In this phase of the technical development, the training partner again is a very important element of the equation. To a certain extent, your training partner should be at least as skillful as you are and, in a perfect world, a much better Jiu-Jitsu practitioner. Why? Simply because he is the individual who needs to set the environment for you and needs to think ahead of your technique. He is the person who will set the circumstances for you to improve your game.

Ideally, your training partner should be your instructor/teacher, and that's why private classes are very important at this stage. Only someone with more understanding, skill and knowledge than you can truly take you to the higher levels of this phase. No beginner will improve your technique at this level. Only someone with a deep and mature understanding of the art, its principles and the complete spectrum of the training phases in the art will be capable of getting the best out of you.

"Only someone with a deep and mature understanding of the art will be capable of getting the best of you."

4) Functionalize: At this level the practitioner already has a) a sound technical foundation; b) a deep understanding of the fundamental principles that rule that specific technique and; c) the ability and precise body feel to use it against different kinds of opponents. Now he needs to kick it up another notch and develop a plan of how to use the given technique against different opponents (size, weight, and physical characteristics). Then he should begin to incorporate combination attacks that involve the study and analysis of how to interrelate and combine that specific movement with other techniques, creating a network of technical solutions.

Each one of the techniques composing that network should have been taken to the master level. Otherwise the technical network will have important flaws that will bring problems to the practitioner. For instance, let's take the triangle as the main technique. You have to learn to adapt this movement against someone who is skinny and against someone who is heavy with a strong neck and shoulder muscles that will impede the movement. Then you must study how to interrelate that movement with, for instance, the straight armlock and *omoplata*.

Now that you have three different options from one single given point in combat, you'll have to be able to attack with one and, as soon as your opponent counters this one, move into the other successively, creating a constant menace for him. He will be only humanly capable of covering a limited amount of attacks. When one door closes, another opens. It is this stage, where you develop a complete game plan, that brings together the fine skill in techniques with the proper tactics and strategies of when and how to use the technique against any kind of opponent and under any kind of situation. To reach this very advanced level, the student needs to be able to modify the techniques against different opponents and combine it with others to create a tactical network. It is only here when you can really say that your Jiu-Jitsu techniques are truly functional.

Unfortunately, and due mostly to today's "fast-food" mentality, the urgency of passing belt tests or winning sport competitions, these phases are overlooked and easily forgotten in many Brazilian Jiu-Jitsu schools. It is true that using the four-phase approach you can become a world champion anyway. But if this happens, it isn't because you found a "shortcut" to excellence. Instead you cut yourself short in your true Jiu-Jitsu potential, allowing a great deal of understanding and talent to be lost somewhere along the way. The road you'll take will depend on the degree of personal imperfection for which you're willing to settle.

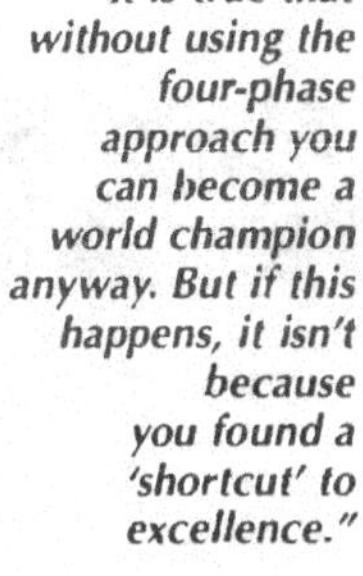

"It is true that without using the four-phase approach you can become a world champion anyway. But if this happens, it isn't because you found a 'shortcut' to excellence."

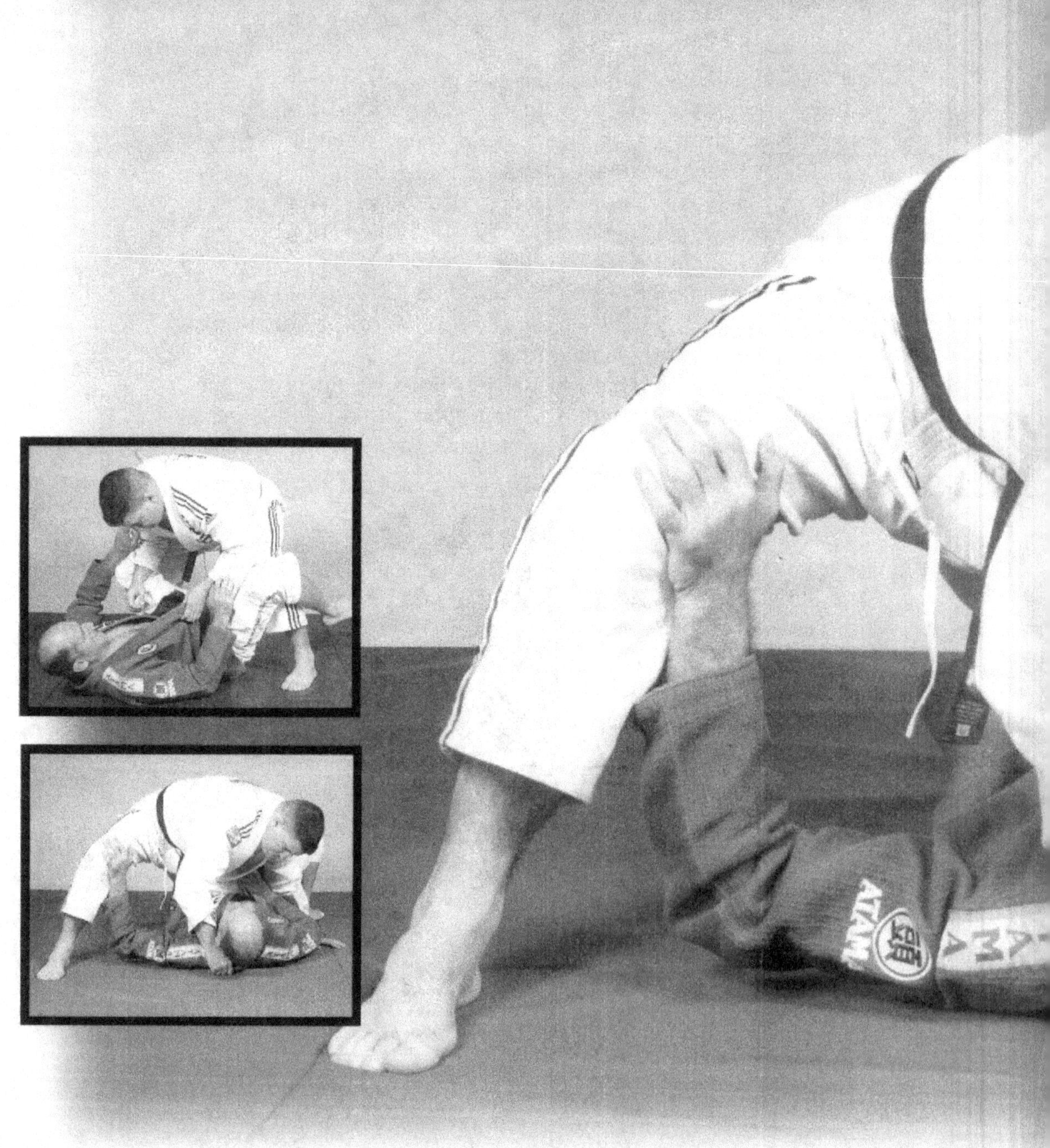

PASSING THE GUARD

VOL. 2

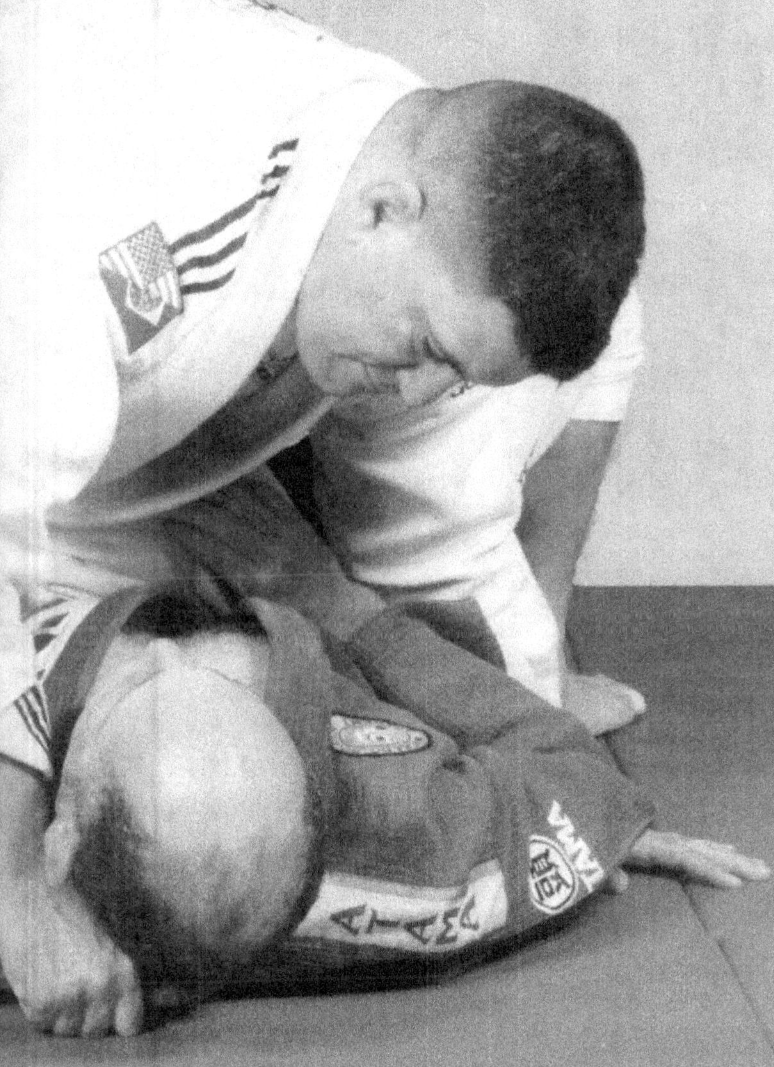

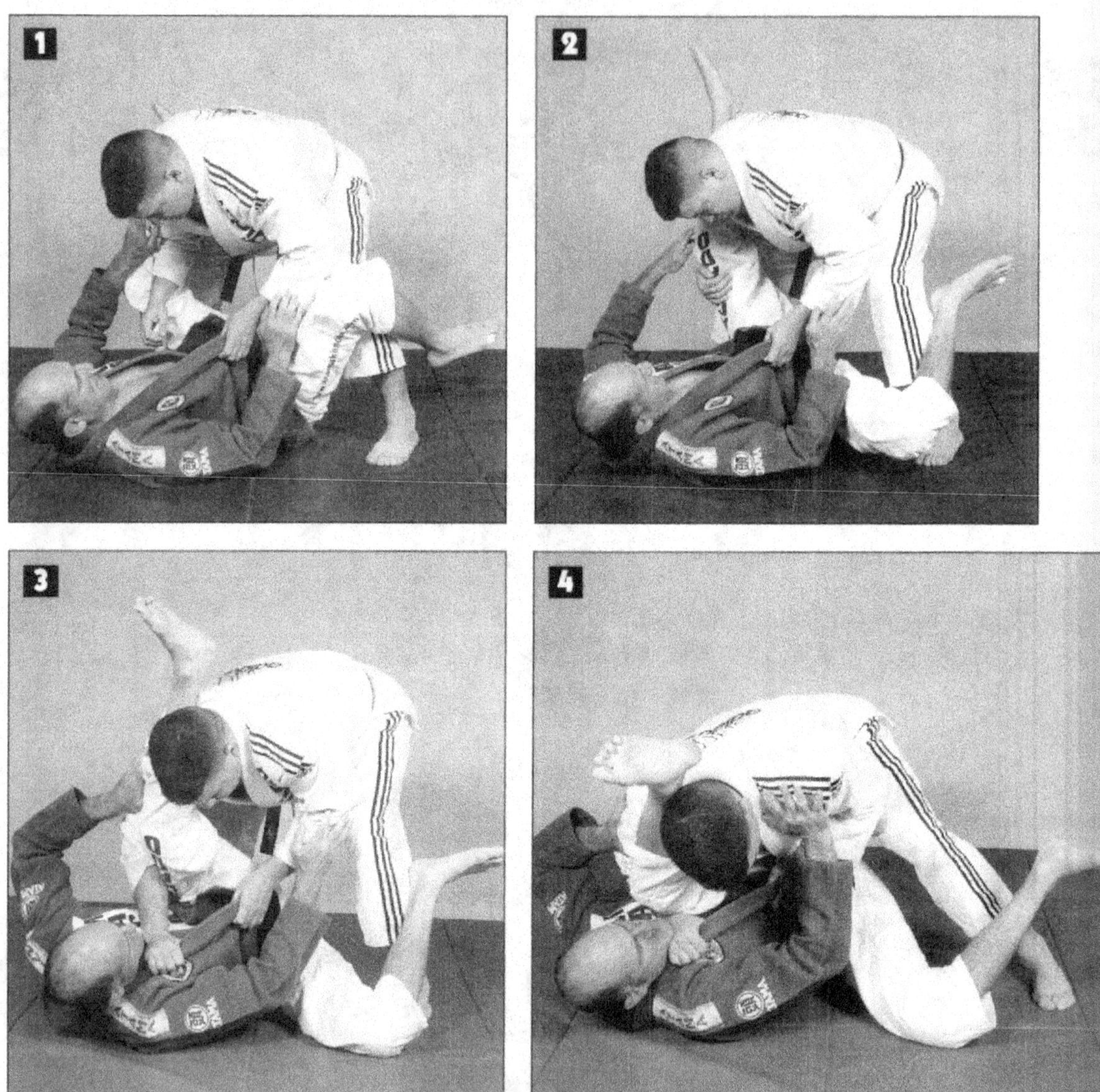

Rigan begins against the opponent's open guard (1). Keeping his left hand on the opponent's gi, Rigan passes his right hand around the outside of the opponent's left leg (2), reaches the upper part of the jacket on the opposite side (3), leans forward and creates pressure (4).

Passing The Guard 1

Now the opponent's left leg is an awkward and uncomfortable position. Rigan twists his body, while maintaining a firm hold (5), and controls the opponent from the side (6).

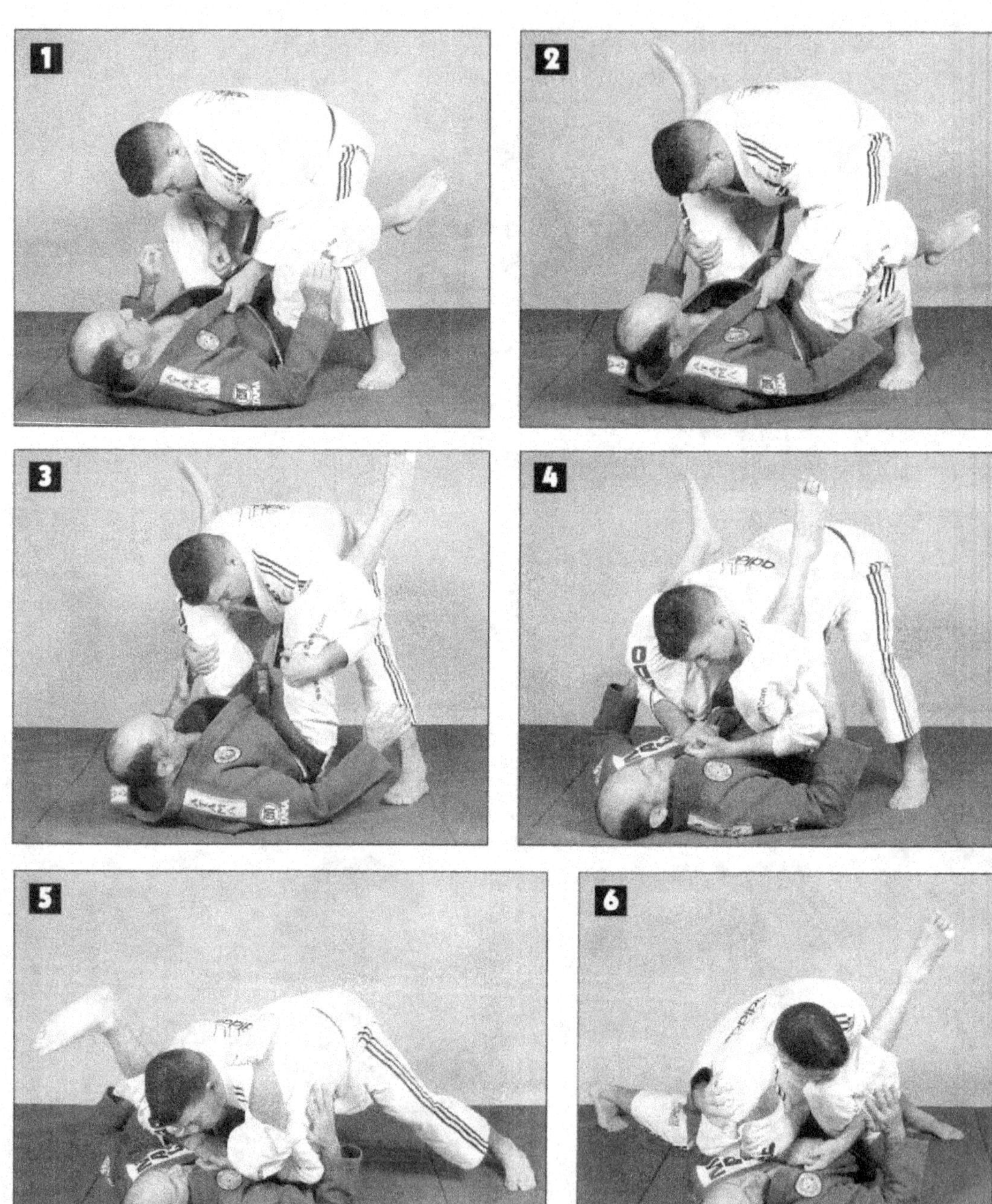

Passing The Guard 2

Rigan faces the opponent's open guard (1). Keeping his left hand firmly on the opponent's gi, Rigan first passes his right hand around the outside of the opponent's left leg and holds on (2). He does the same thing on the other side with his left hand. Now he has both legs (3). Rigan starts leaning forward and clutches his hands together (4). He continues leaning forward until he feels the opportunity to twist his body (5-6). This enables him to pass the guard and assume the side control position for taking the offensive (7).

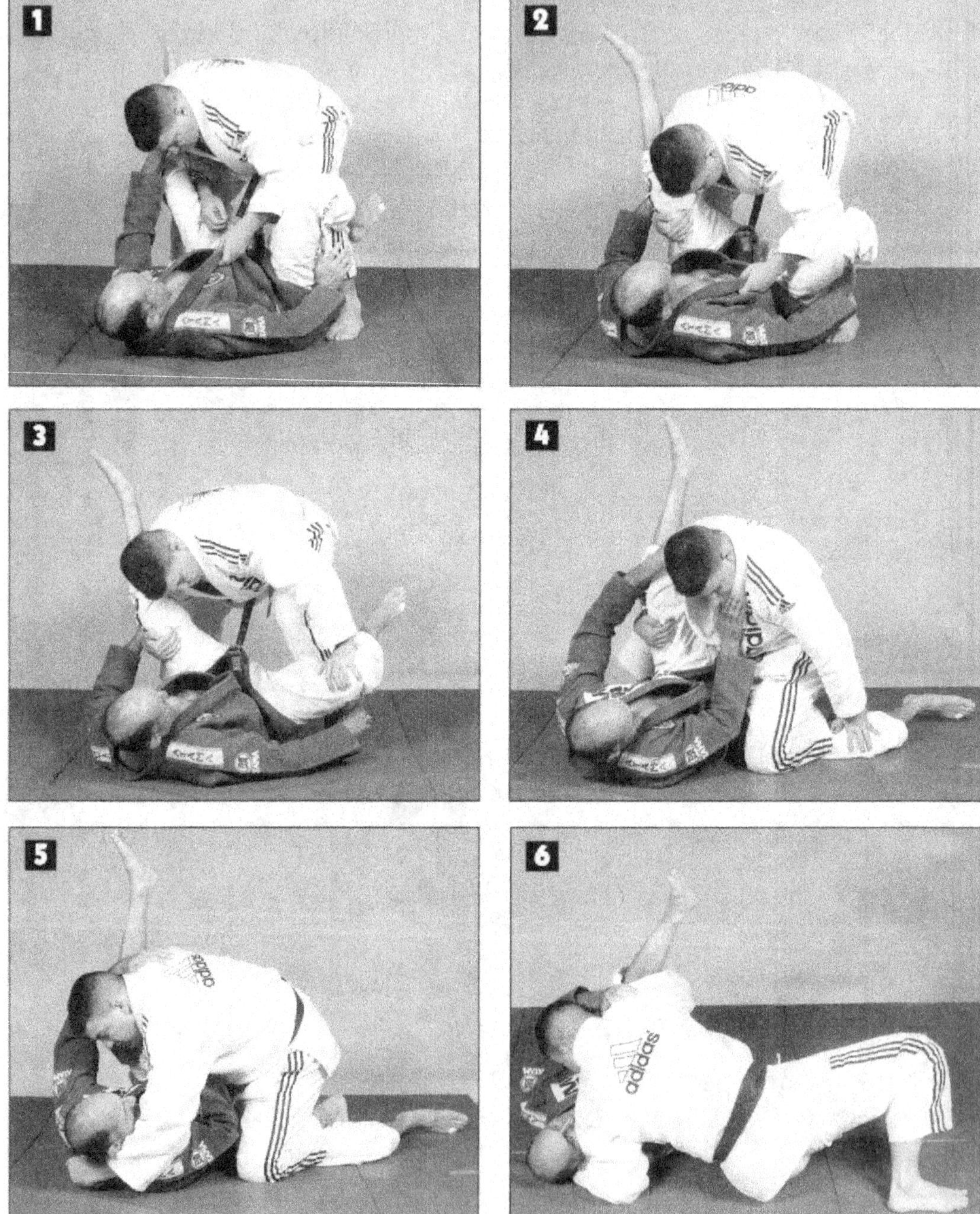

Passing The Guard 3

Rigan begins against the opponent's open guard (1). Keeping his left hand securely on the opponent's gi, Rigan passes his right hand around the outside of the left leg, grabs on and simultaneously puts pressure on the opponent's right leg with his left elbow (2). Note how that opens the leg. Next, Rigan simply uses his left hand to push the leg down (3) and then passes his left knee over the opponent's right leg (4). To establish himself, Rigan uses his left hand to reach the back of the opponent's collar (5). He then brings his right leg all the way back to pass the guard (6). Finally, Rigan switches the positions of his legs to gain side control (7).

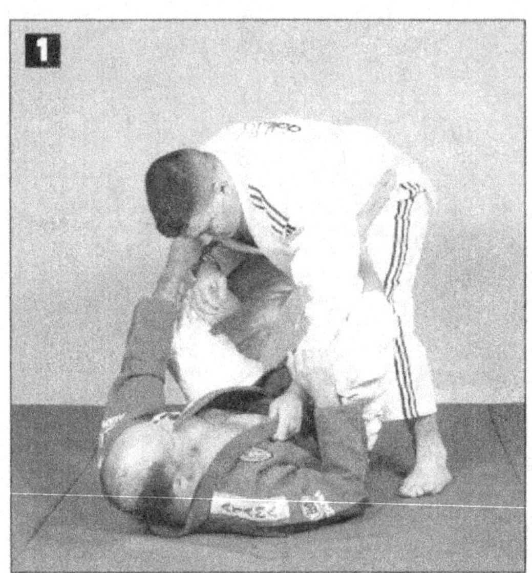 

Rigan faces the opponent's open guard (1). While grabbing the gi with his left hand, Rigan uses his right hand to grab the opponent's right pants leg (2). He then immediately does the same thing with his left hand (3). Rigan moves to the right and pushes both of the opponent's legs to the left side (4).

Passing The Guard 4

He slides his left leg close to the opponent's left side (5) and takes the offensive from a side control (6).

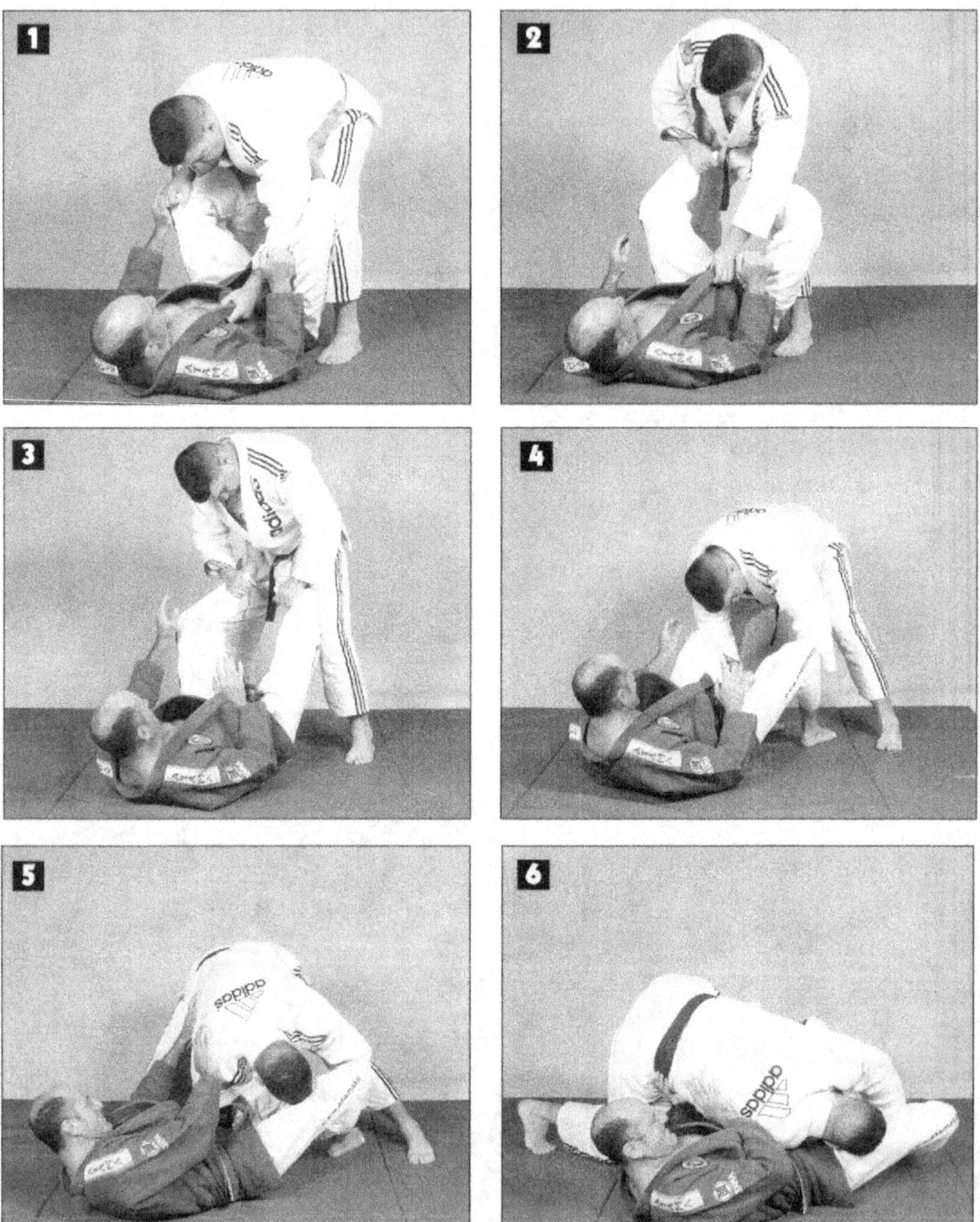

Passing The Guard 5

Rigan faces the opponent's open guard (1). While keeping his left hand on the opponent's gi, Rigan uses his right hand to grab the lower part of the opponent's pants (2). Rigan then immediately does the same thing with the left hand (3). Rigan pushes both legs to the floor (4), and rolls to the right (5). By keeping constant pressure (6), Rigan assumes full side control (7).

 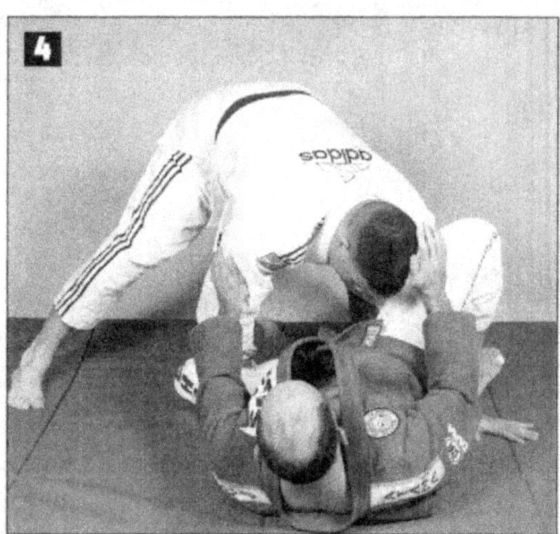

Rigan faces the opponent's open guard (1). Keeping his left hand firmly on the opponent's gi, Rigan grabs his opponent's pants with his right hand (2). Rigan pushes the right leg down (3), and moves his right leg to the side so he can circle around the opponent's left leg (4).

Passing The Guard **6** A

Using his left leg to help to control the opponent's left leg (5), Rigan moves carefully to the side (6), where he brings his knees up to control the position (7). Now he can start his offensive from the side (8).

Side View of Previous Technique

From this angle, we can see how Rigan pushes his opponent's leg all the way to the floor (1-2). By moving his hips to the right, Rigan avoids the opponent's guard (3-4).

Passing The Guard **6** B

Note that Rigan's right hand is in full control of the opponent's left leg until Rigan brings his knee forward (5). This allows him to move into side control (6).

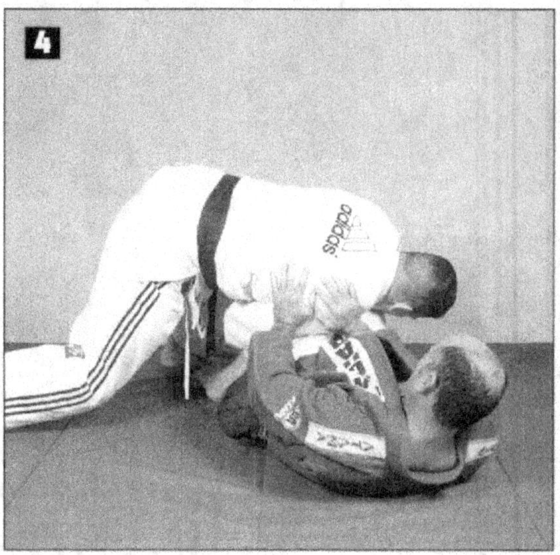

Rigan faces the opponent's open guard. Keeping his left hand firmly on the opponent's gi, Rigan uses his right hand to grab the lower part of the opponent's pants. He immediately does the same thing with the left hand (1-2). Rigan then pushes both legs directly to the floor (3).

Passing The Guard 7

Next he rolls over the opponent (4-5). This allows him to rotate 360 degrees (6) until he assumes side control (7).

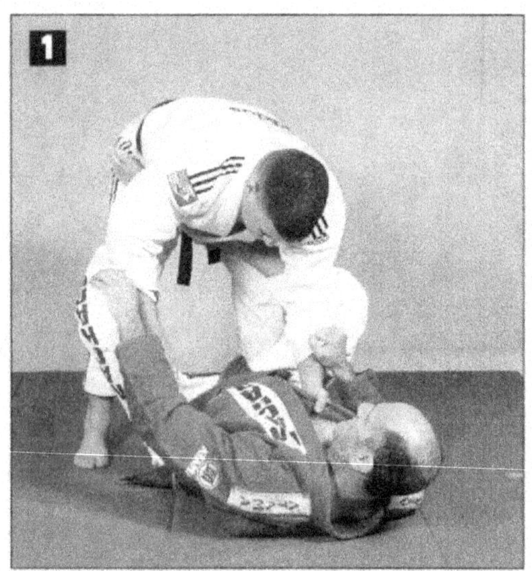

Rigan faces the opponent's open guard (1). Keeping his left hand on the opponent's gi, Rigan uses his right hand to grab the opponent's left ankle (2). Using his left hand, he clamps onto the opponent's right ankle (3). Rigan pushes both ankles down (4) until they reach the point in

Passing The Guard 8

which he can bring his hips forward (5), and trap both legs by lowering his body to the ground (6).

continued

continued from page 19

Now inside the opponent's
guard (7), Rigan controls the
opponent's left leg with his
right arm (8), and moves his
hips to the outside, securing
the leg with his right hand (9).

Passing The Guard 8

When he feels comfortable and confident (10), he releases the grip and secures the position with his left knee from the side (11).

Rigan faces the opponent's open guard (1). Keeping his left hand on the opponent's gi, Rigan lowers his body while permitting his opponent to keep his left knee up (2). Rigan uses this to his advantage because he can apply pressure to the left leg (3). Rigan then passes over the opponent's right leg (4). Once comfortable with the control, Rigan uses his right knee to pass the guard (5).

Passing The Guard 9

He quickly assumes side control so he can initiate the attack (6). When you use your right knee to pass over the opponent's right leg, use your left foot to hook his leg. This will prevent him from reversing the movement and putting you inside his guard. The left foot secures the move until the right knee passes the opponent's right leg.

Rigan encounters the opponent's open guard (1). Rigan grabs his opponent's pants with his left hand, applies pressure and moves to the left (2). Then he pulls the left leg all the way up, unbalancing the opponent and preventing him from countering (3).

Passing The Guard **10**

Rigan pushes the leg away from him while keeping his left leg close to the opponent (4). He immediately releases the leg and places his right knee on the opponent's chest for a knee side control (5).

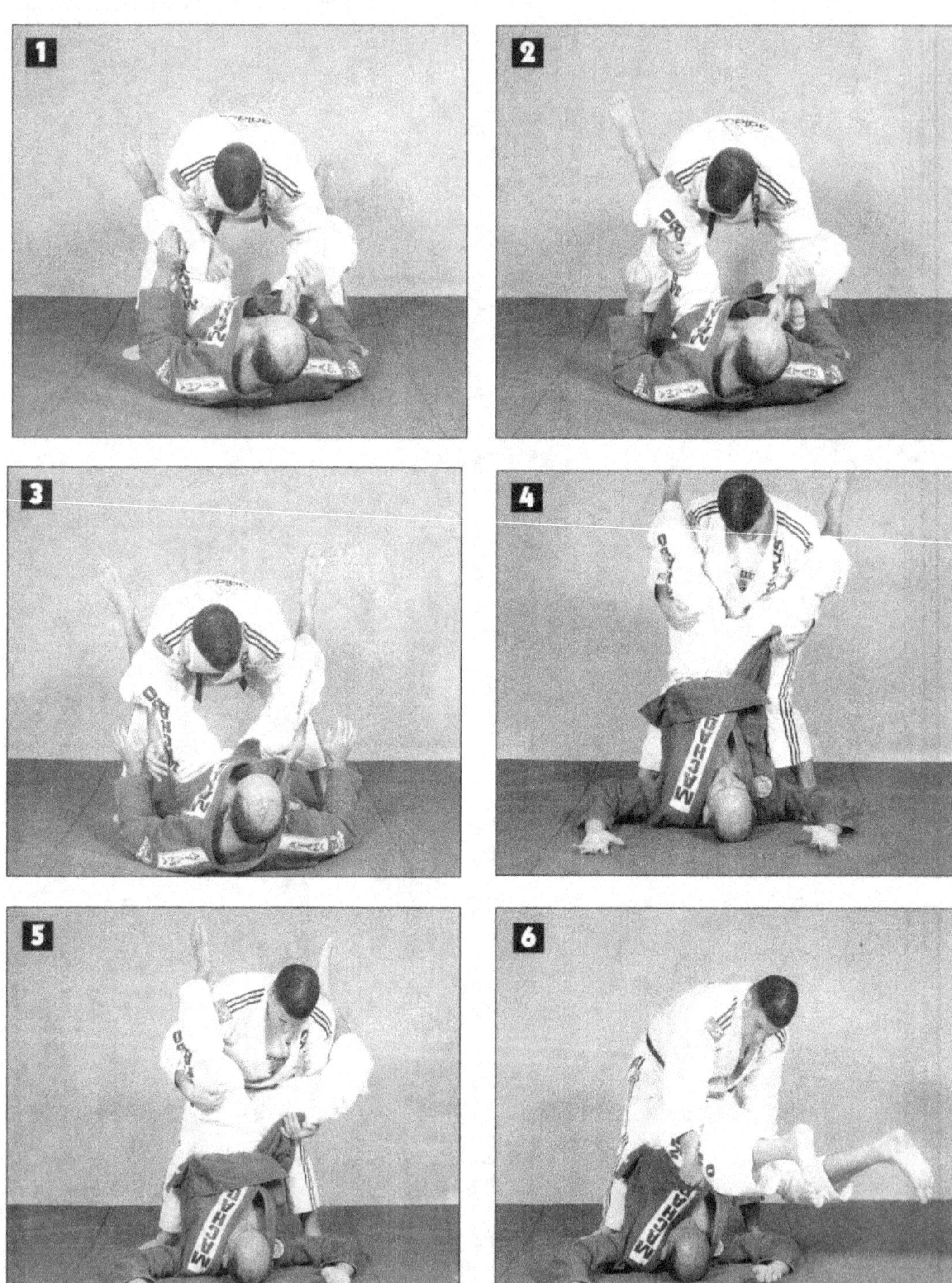

Passing The Guard 11

Rigan faces the opponent's open guard (1). Keeping his left hand on the opponent's gi, Rigan passes his right hand around the left leg (2). He then does the same thing on the other side with his left hand (3). Rigan pulls both legs up (4), and pushes forward with his hips to completely unbalance the opponent (5). Rigan pushes the legs to the left (6).

Next, Rigan tries to establish better control (7), but the opponent rolls and tries to escape (8). Rigan reacts by controlling him from the back (9).

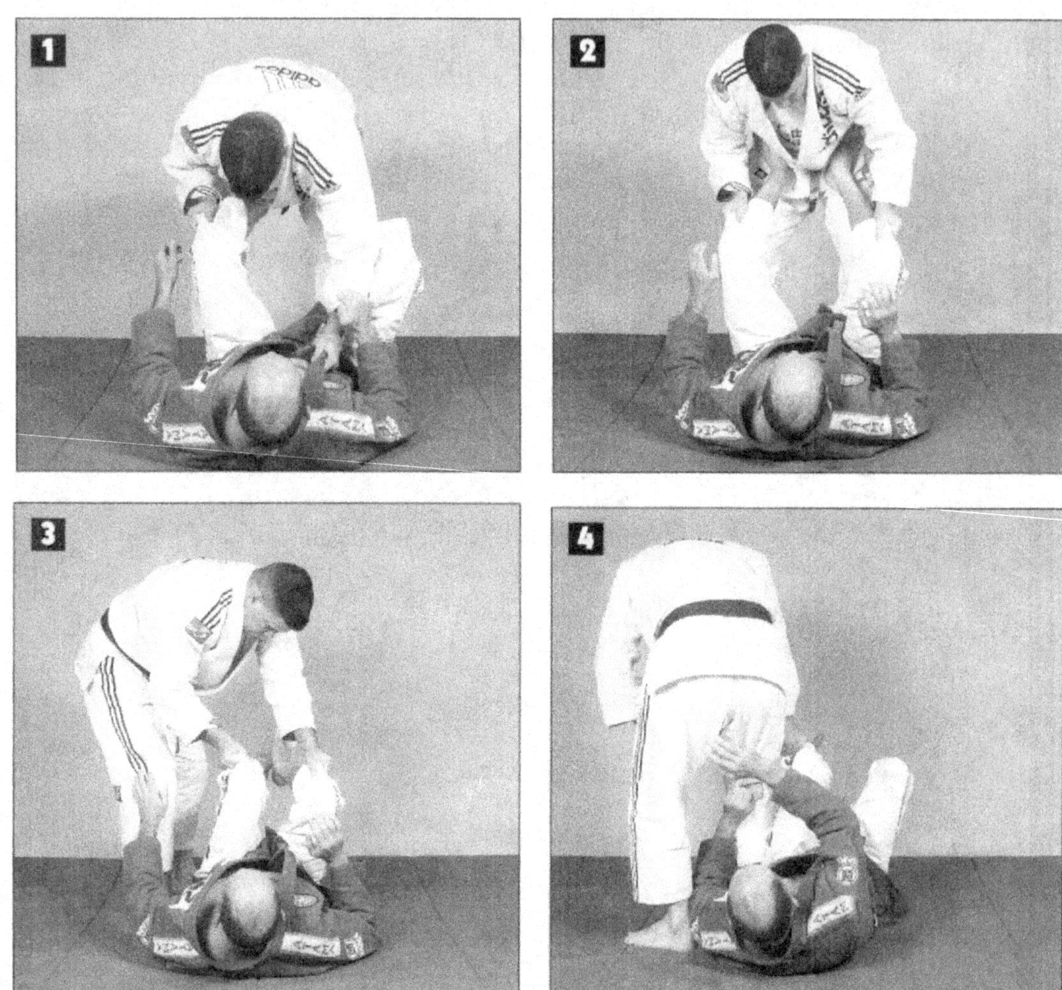

Rigan faces the opponent's open guard (1). He releases the opponent's gi and quickly grabs the pants (2). Rigan pulls hard with both hands to nullify the opponent's guard (3).

Passing The Guard **12**

Rigan turns 360 degrees (4-5), and assumes the knee side control (6).

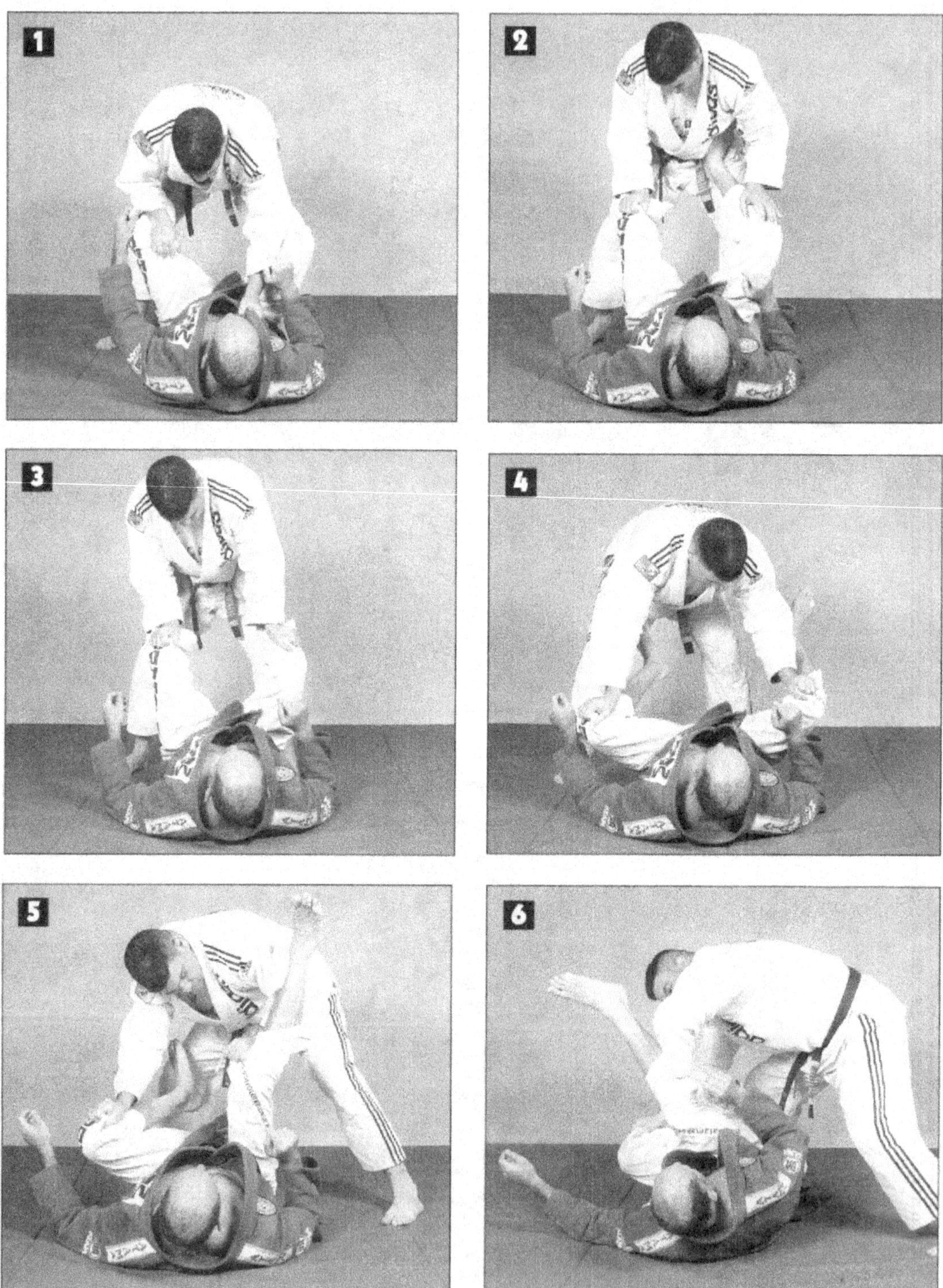

Passing The Guard 13

Rigan faces the opponent's open guard (1). He changes grips and moves his left hand to the opponent's pants (2). Once both hands are controlling the opponent's pants (3), Rigan opens the legs by pushing them out (4). Rigan immediately turns and moves to his left (5), using his left elbow to keep the pressure on and pass the guard (6).

Maintaining control by adding pressure with his left hand (7), Rigan drops to the ground and uses his left side for initial control (8). Then he completes the movement (9).

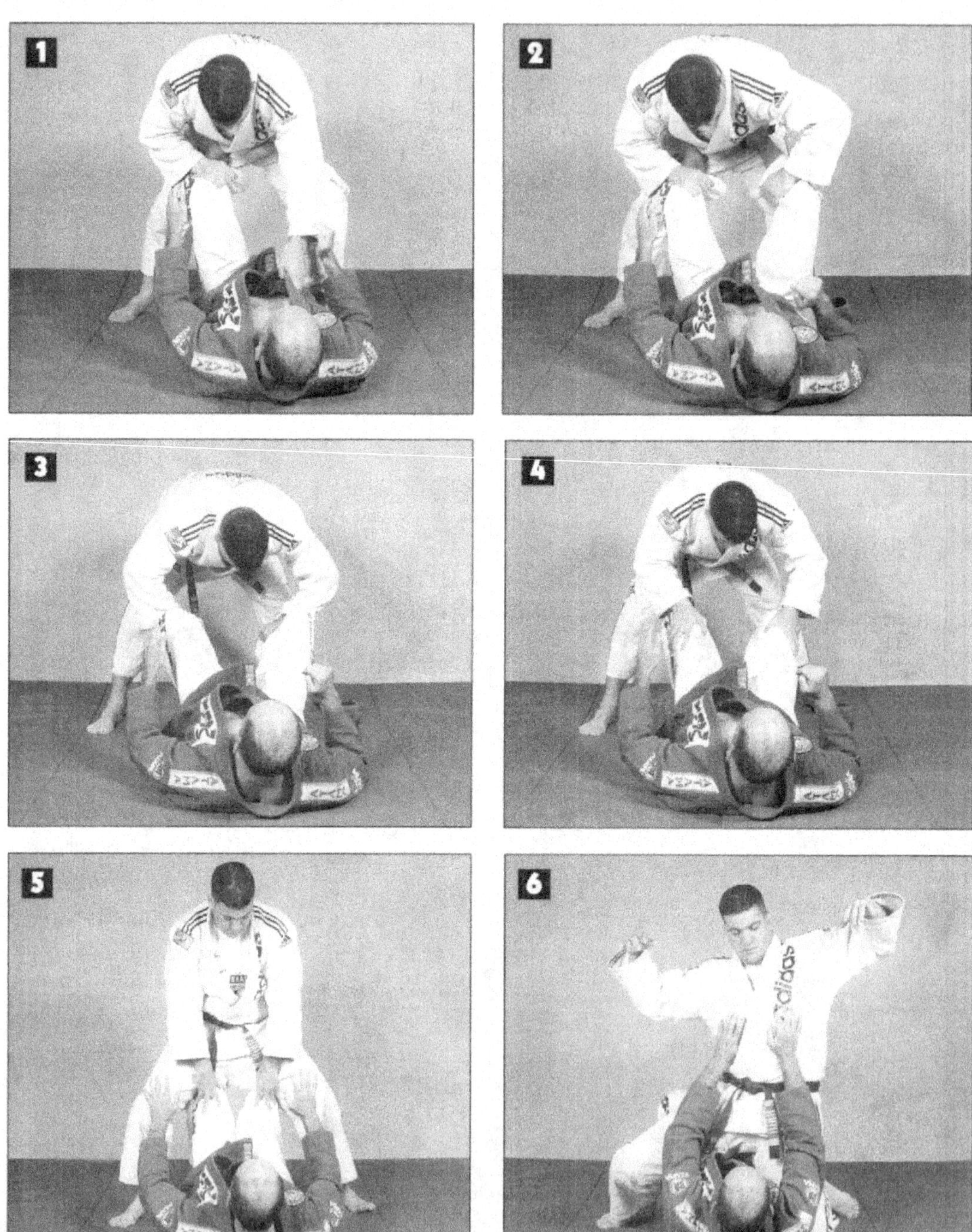

Passing The Guard 14

Rigan faces the opponent's open guard (1). He again changes grips and moves his left hand to the opponent's pants (2). Once both hands are controlling the opponent's pants (3), Rigan releases his grip, pushes down (4-5), leans forward (6), and mounts the opponent (7).

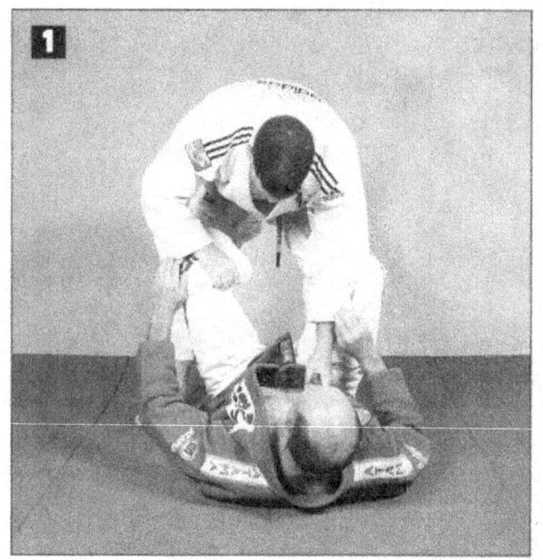

Rigan faces the opponent's open
guard (1). He releases his opponent's
gi and puts his left hand on the
ground (2). This creates support to
push himself up (3), and spin

Passing The Guard **15**

in the air (4). He lands on the other side, where he controls the opponent from the side (5).

Rigan faces the opponent's open guard (1). He moves his left leg slightly backward to create space (2), and then he places it between the opponent's legs (3), putting pressure over the left thigh (4). By sliding his hips down to the right side (5),

Passing The Guard 16

Rigan passes the guard (6), and assumes full side control (7).

Rigan faces the opponent's open guard (1). By moving his body backward, he creates space (2) to circle around with his right leg (3). Rigan sits on the ground, but he maintains tight control on the opponent's left leg (4-5)

Passing The Guard 17

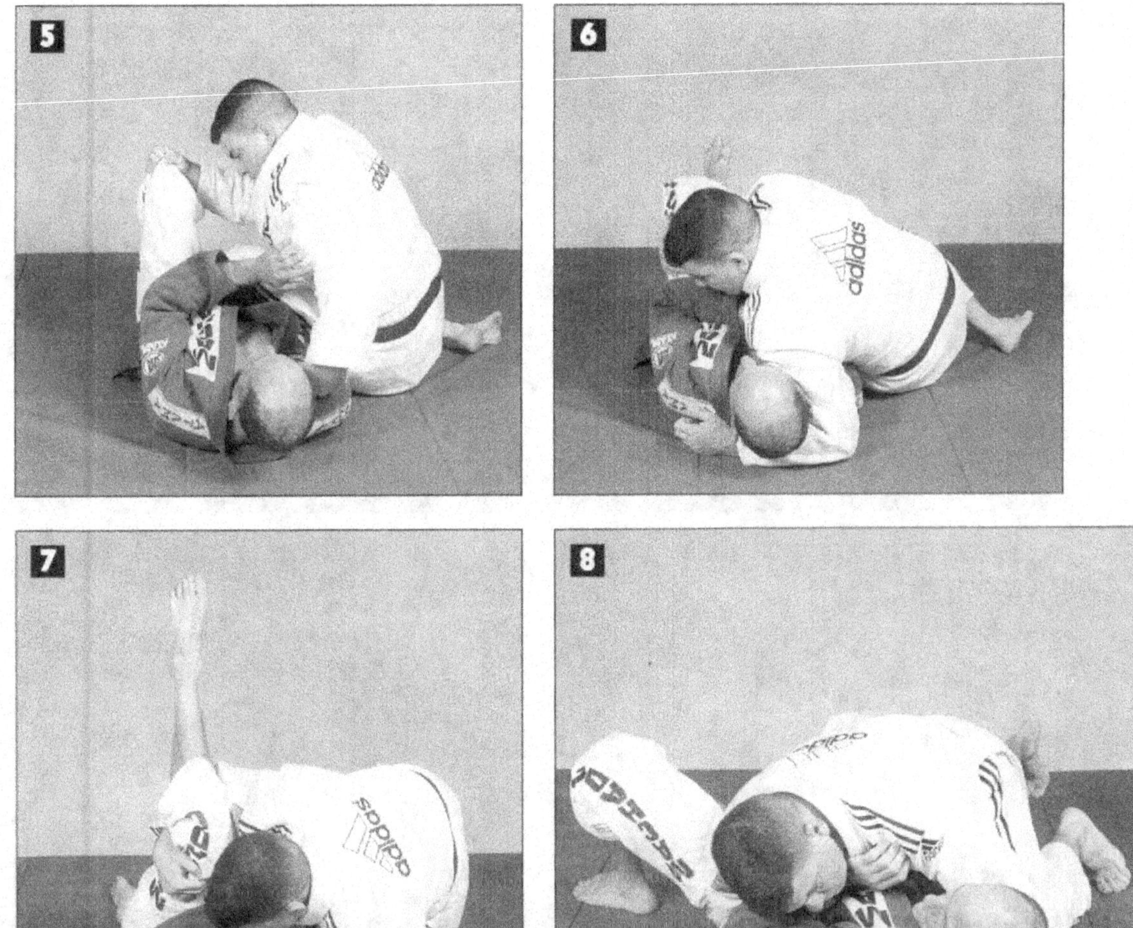

until he feels comfortable to move his hips (6), and left leg out (7). He then assumes full side control (8).

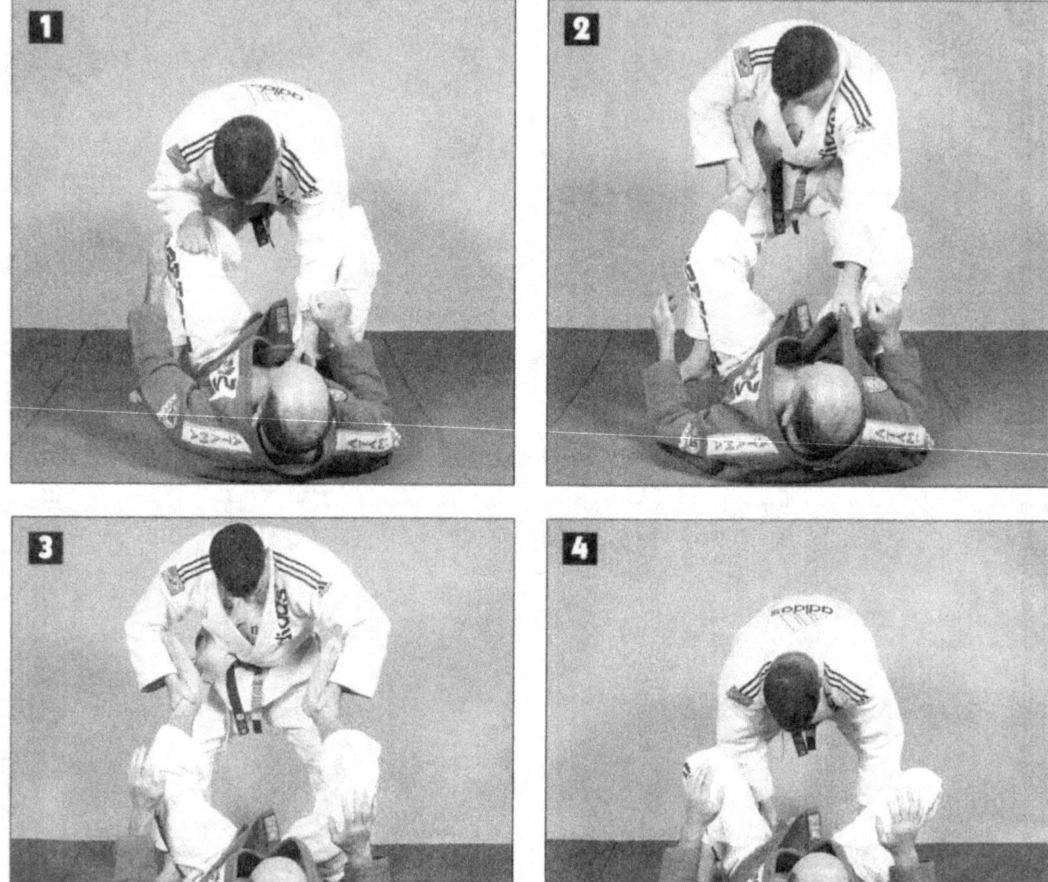

Rigan faces the opponent's open guard (1). Keeping his left hand firmly on the opponent's gi, he uses his right hand to grab the opponent's left ankle (2). He then releases the gi and grabs the opponent's right ankle (3). Rigan pushes both ankles down (4) until they reach the point in which he can

Passing The Guard **18**

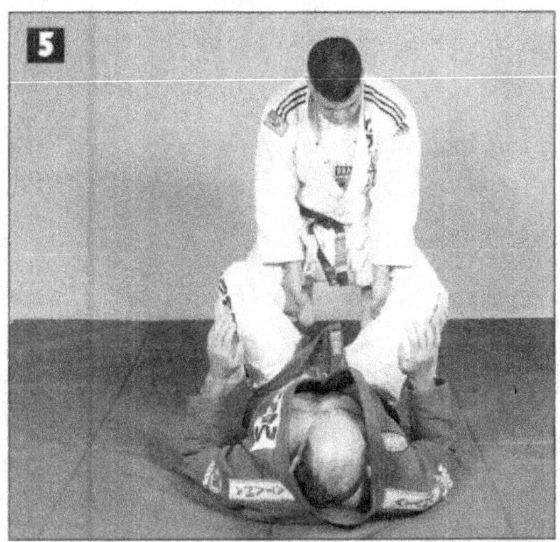

bring his hips forward (5). He then traps both legs by lowering his own body to the ground (6). Now inside the opponent's guard (7), Rigan moves to the left and uses both hands to support himself (8).

continued

continued from page 41

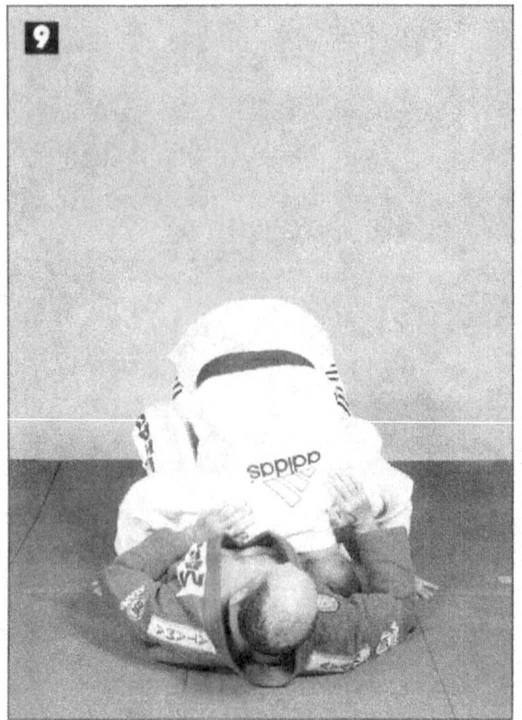

He pushes up (9) and thrusts his body into the air (10). He spins and lands with both feet on the opponent's left (11).

Passing The Guard 18

Reversing his position (12), Rigan assumes side control so he can take the offensive (13).

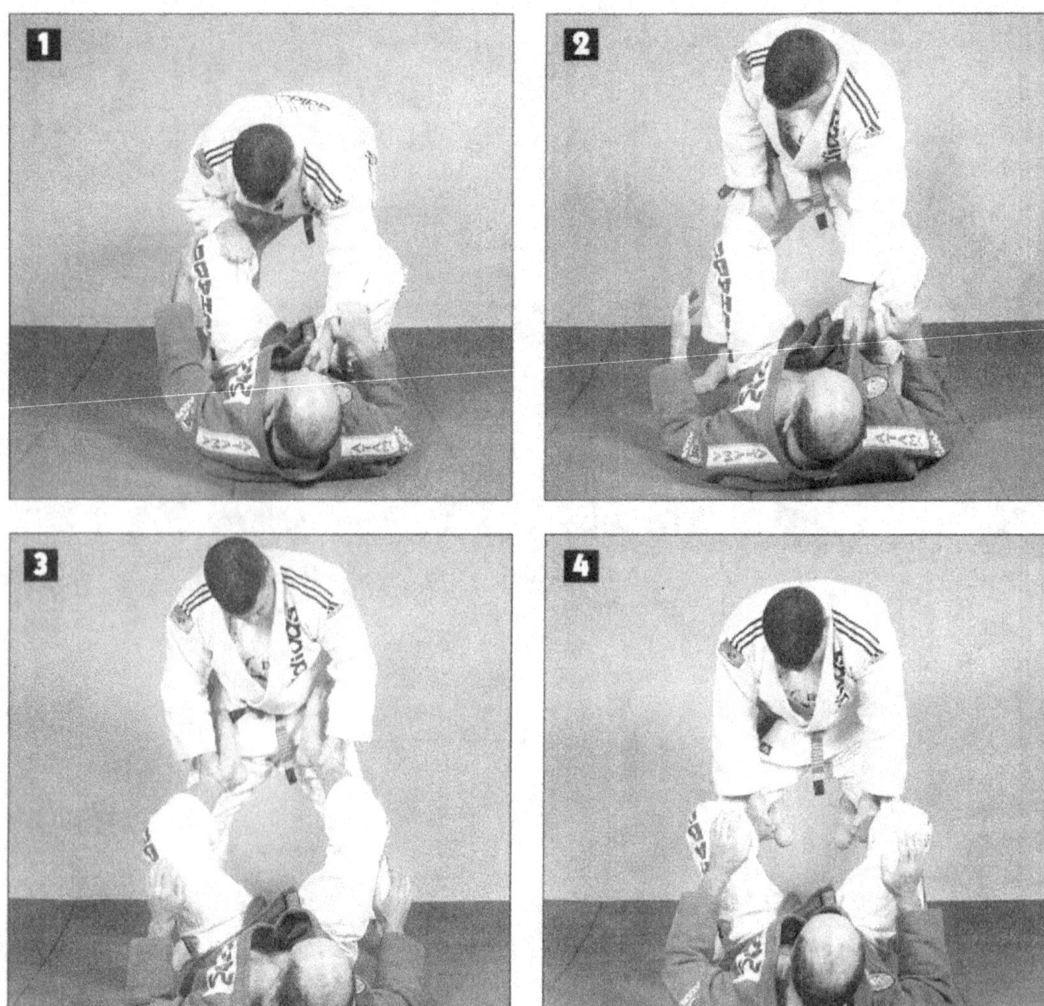

Rigan faces the opponent's open guard (1). Keeping his left hand on the gi, Rigan uses his right hand to grab the opponent's left ankle (2). He releases the gi with his left hand and grabs the opponent's right ankle (3). Rigan pushes both ankles down (4), until they reach the point that he can bring

Passing The Guard **19**

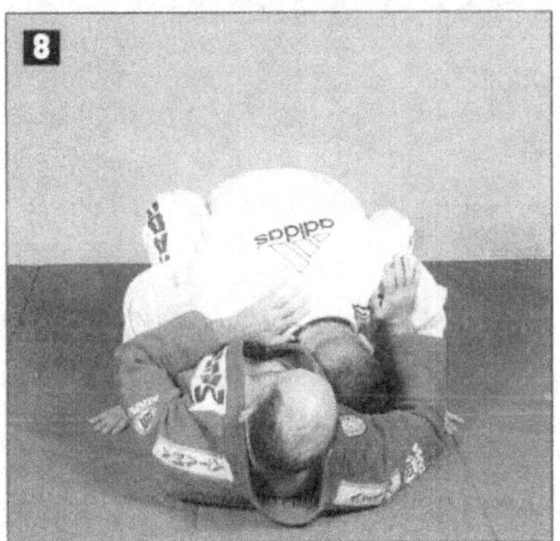

his hips forward (5). He traps both legs by lowering his body to the ground
(6). Now inside the opponent's guard (7), Rigan moves to the left and uses
both hands to support himself (8).

continued

continued from page 45

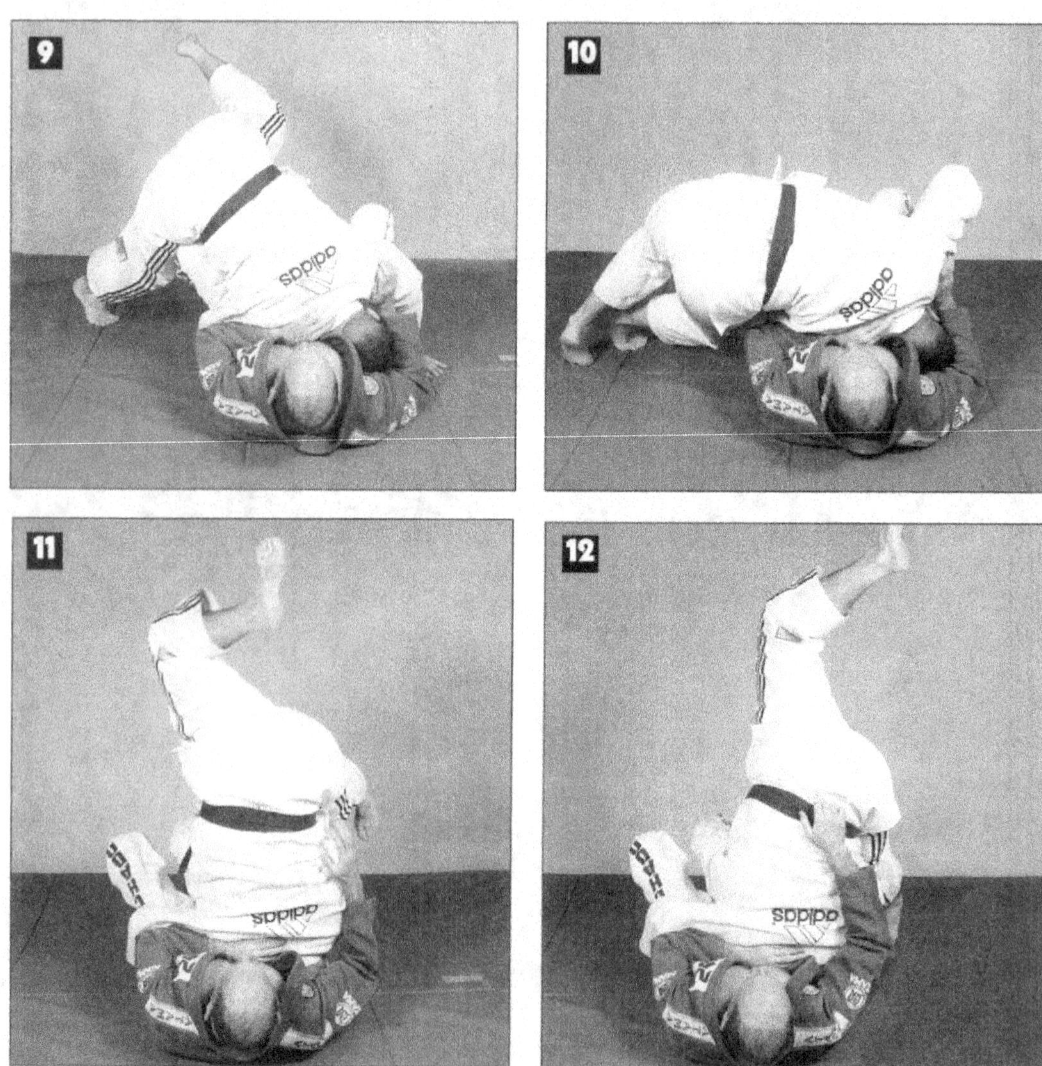

Rigan uses his right hand to prevent the opponent from using his left leg to put him back in the guard (9-10). Rigan gathers momentum and pushes himself to the opposite side (11-12).

Passing The Guard 19

Here he switches his position (13), and goes for the final side control (14-15).

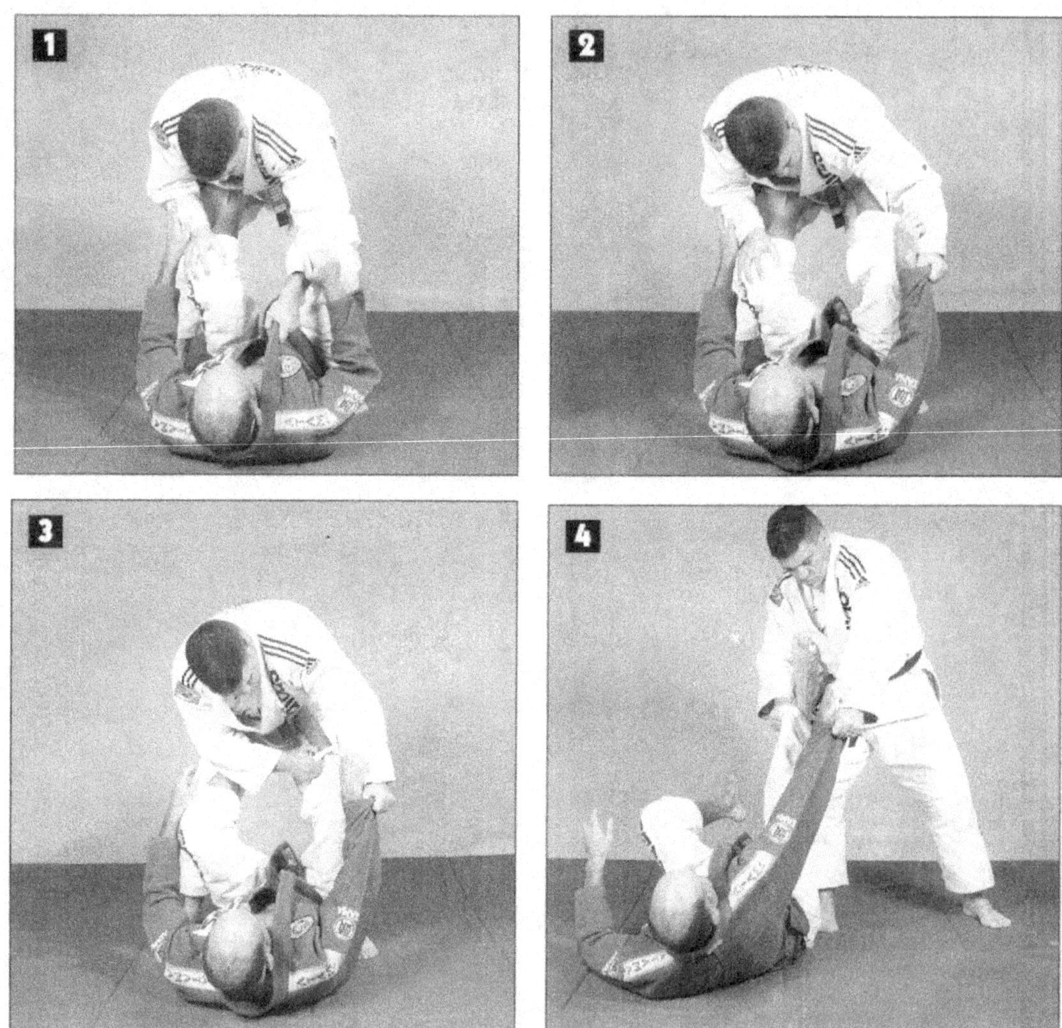

While facing his opponent's open guard, Rigan grabs his opponent's gi (1). Then he moves his grip to the opponent's right sleeve (2), as his right hand moves to the right leg (3). Rigan pulls hard and moves around the opponent (4), which enables him to avoid the guard (5).

Passing The Guard 20

Rigan then places his right knee on the chest for a full side control (6). It is critical to maintain control of the opponent's right leg and sleeve during these moves because this will enable you to avoid the guard or an attack.

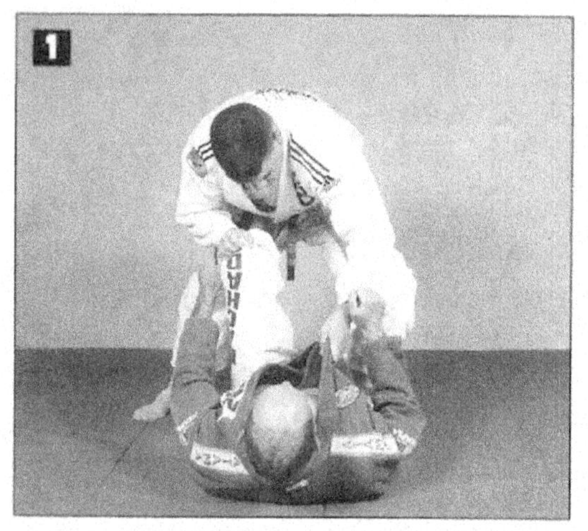
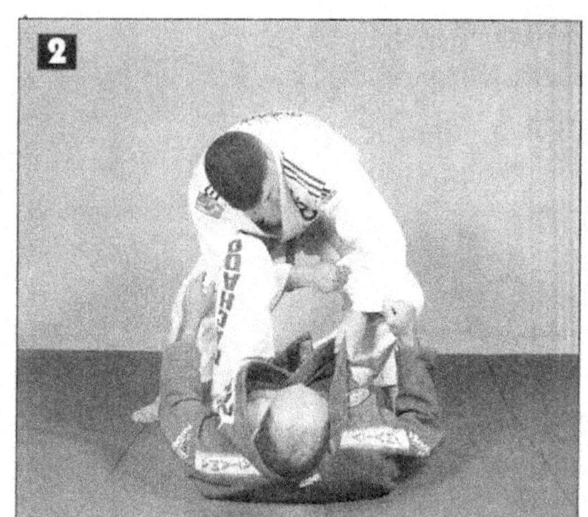

Passing The Guard 21

Rigan faces the opponent's open guard with his left hand securely on the gi (1).
He passes his right hand under the opponent's left leg so he can grab the opponent's right leg (2). He does the same thing on the other side with his left hand
(3). He lowers both legs (4-5), rolls to the right and passes the guard (6-7).

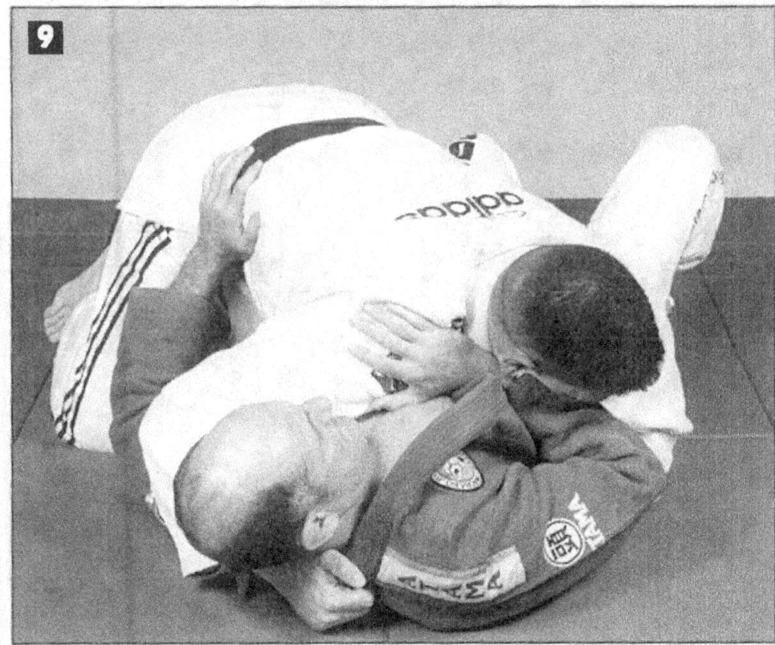

Now he can control the opponent completely (8-9).

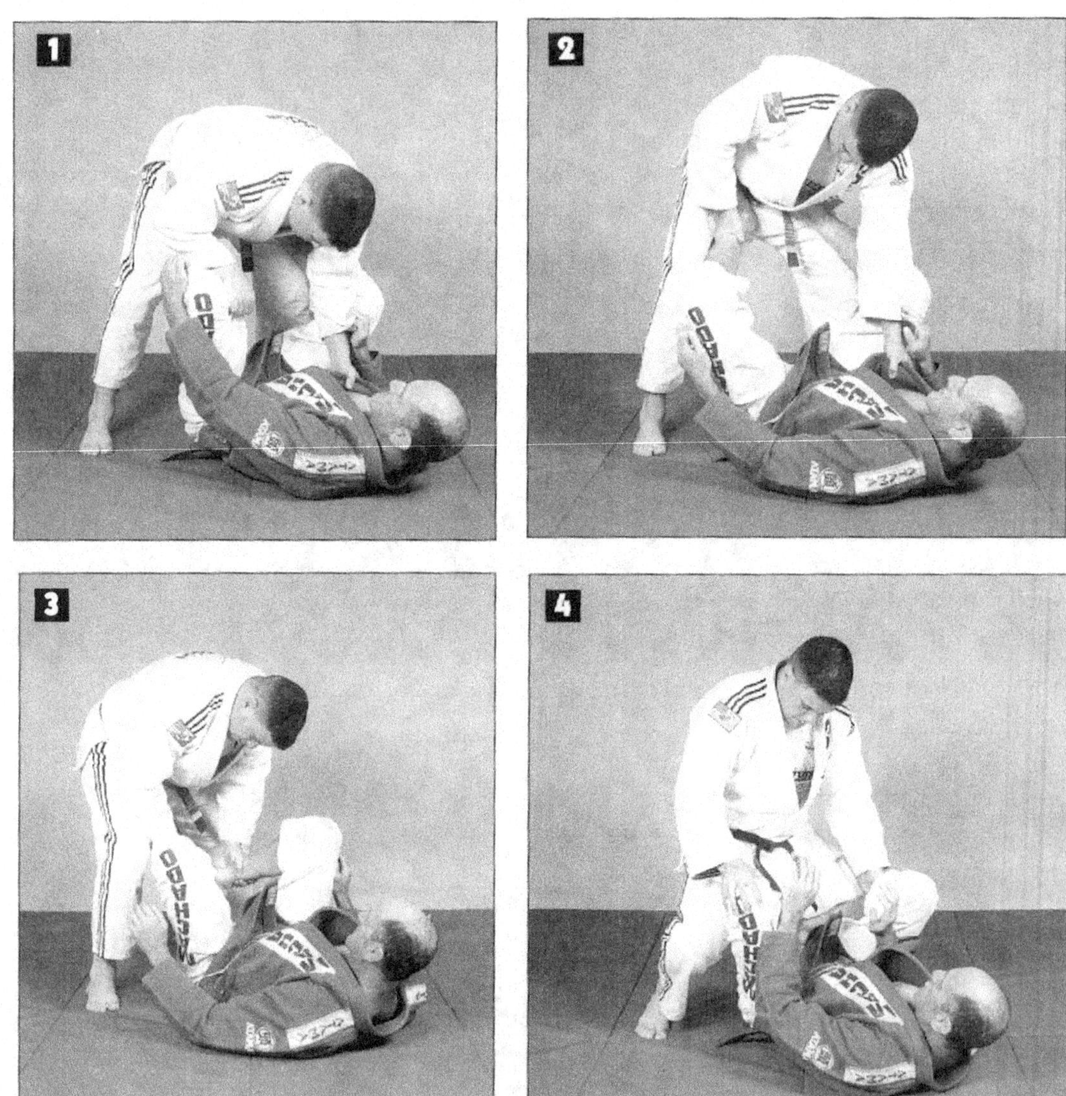

Rigan faces the opponent's open guard (1). Keeping his left hand firmly on the gi, Rigan uses his right hand to grab the opponent's left ankle (2). He does the same with his left hand on the opponent's right ankle (3). Rigan pushes both legs down (4).

Passing The Guard **22**

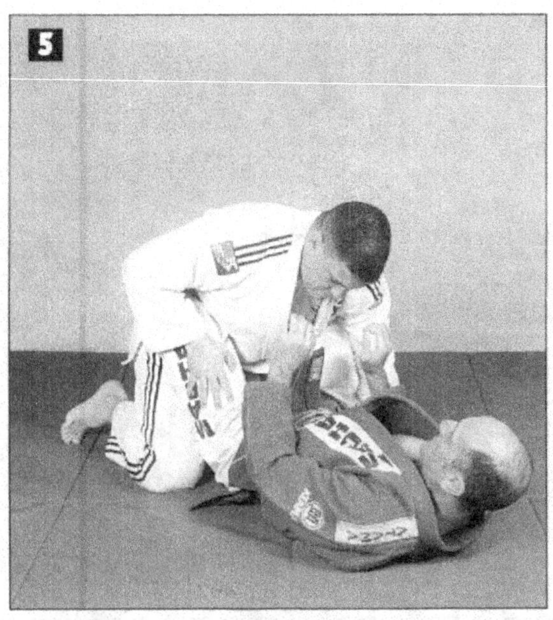

When they reach the point where he can bring his hips forward (5), he traps both legs with his body (6).

continued

continued from page 53

He swings his left leg to his
right side (7) and then reverses
the position of his legs (8) to
pass his right leg outside the
opponent's left side (9).

Passing The Guard **22**

For better positioning, he again switches the position of his legs (10), turns and assumes side control (11).

Rigan grabs both of his opponent's legs (1). By pushing forward with his hips and hands, Rigan adds pressure to the opponent's back, preventing him from escaping (2-3). Rigan maintains the pressure by continuing to push forward (4).

Passing The Guard **23**

As soon as he feels the opportunity, Rigan grabs the opponent's collar under the neck with his right hand (5) and starts passing the guard (6). He ends up with side control (7).

Rigan faces the opponent's open guard (1). He uses his right hand to grab the opponent's left ankle and his left hand to grab the opponent's right ankle (2). Rigan pushes both ankles down (3), until they reach the point where he can bring his hips

Passing The Guard 24

forward (4) and trap both legs by lowering his body to the ground (5).

continued

continued from page 59

Now he "opens" his right leg to the side as he traps the opponent's right leg with his left arm (6). Using the right leg for support, Rigan swings to the other side (7) and now uses his left leg to control the opponent's right leg. This allows him to move his left hand to the back of the collar (8).

Passing The Guard 24

For better control, he again switches the position of his legs. Note how his right leg is over the opponent's right hip. Rigan then assumes side control (9).

Rigan faces the opponent's open
guard (1). He passes his right hand
under the opponent's left leg (2),
and starts leaning forward (3)

Passing The Guard 25

until his knees touch the ground (4). Keeping firm control on the opponent's left hip with his right hand (5),

continued

continued from page 63

Rigan starts moving to his left
so he can pass the guard. Notice
how he keeps a tight grip on the
opponent's collar with his left
hand (6). The opponent tries to
counter by lifting his left leg up
and bringing it to the front (7-8),

Passing The Guard **25**

but Rigan reacts by pulling the opponent's left hip hard with his right hand (9), and moving fast to the left. He then assumes side control (10).

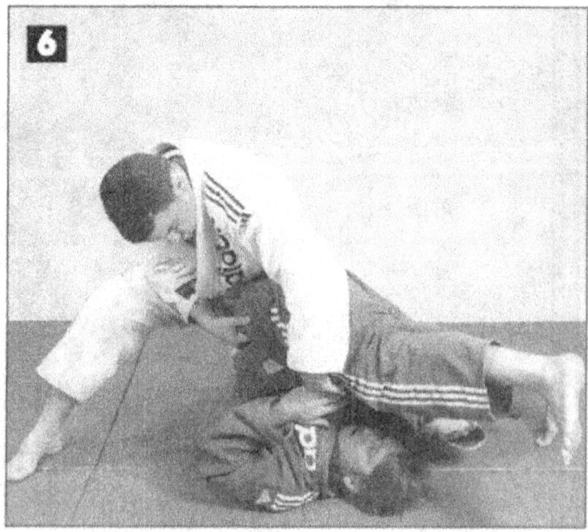

Passing The Guard 26

Rigan faces the opponent's open guard (1). He passes his right hand under the opponent's left leg (2), and he starts leaning forward (3). He grabs the opponent's belt with both hands (4), and pulls hard. This places the opponent in a disadvantageous position (5) to counter Rigan

when he moves to his right (6-8), and passes the guard. Ultimately, Rigan assumes side control (9).

Passing The Guard 27

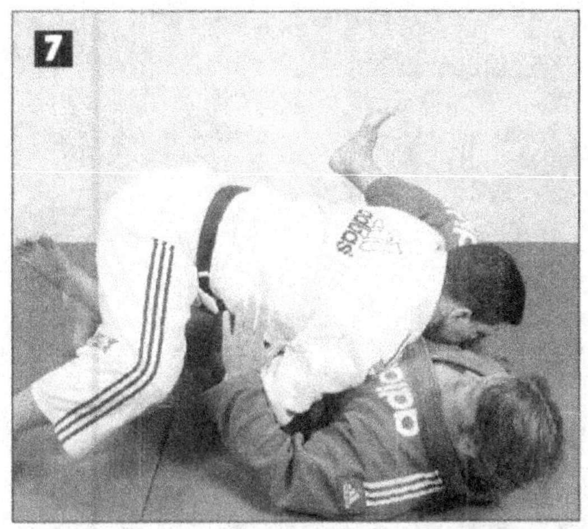

Rigan faces the opponent's open guard (1). He passes his right hand under the opponent's left leg (2), and starts leaning forward (3). Rigan then grabs the opponent's hips with both hands (4), and applies pressure with his body (5) until he finds the right opportunity to pass his right leg over (6) his opponent. Meanwhile, he keeps tight control with his right arm on the opponent's left leg (7). Using this control as a support, he pushes himself in the air (8), and fully passes the opponent's guard (9). From here he assumes side control, where he can then initiate the offensive (10).

Passing The Guard 28

Rigan faces the opponent's open guard and grabs the opponent's pants right above the knee (1). He twists the grip to the inside (2), and begins to push the opponent's left leg with his forearm (3). He immediately releases the grip and grabs the collar (4), which gives him superior position to maintain pressure (5-6)

and move to the right side (7). Here he can pass the guard (8), and assume side control (9).

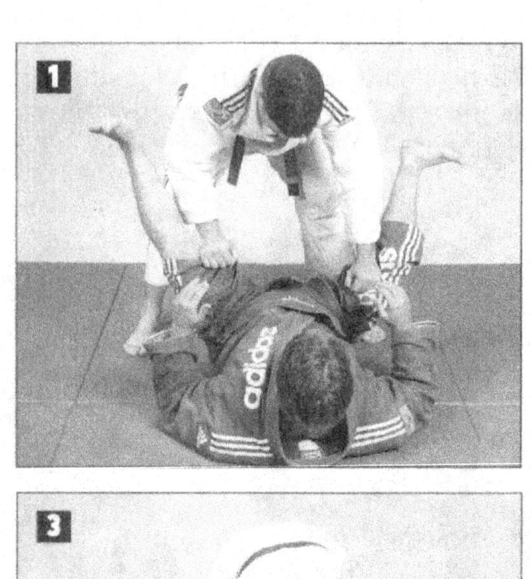

Passing The Guard 29

Rigan faces the open guard and grabs the opponent's pants at the knee (1). He twists the grip to the inside and begins to push the opponent's left leg with his forearm (2). He immediately releases the grip and grabs the collar (3), providing him with superior position to keep the pressure on and move to the left (4). He passes his right leg by lifting it up all the way (5) to the opponent's right side (6). He wraps up the move by taking control from the side (7). It is important to keep a tight grip over the opponent's left leg during the complete movement. This will ensure that he can't bring it up to your head and prevent you from passing to the side.

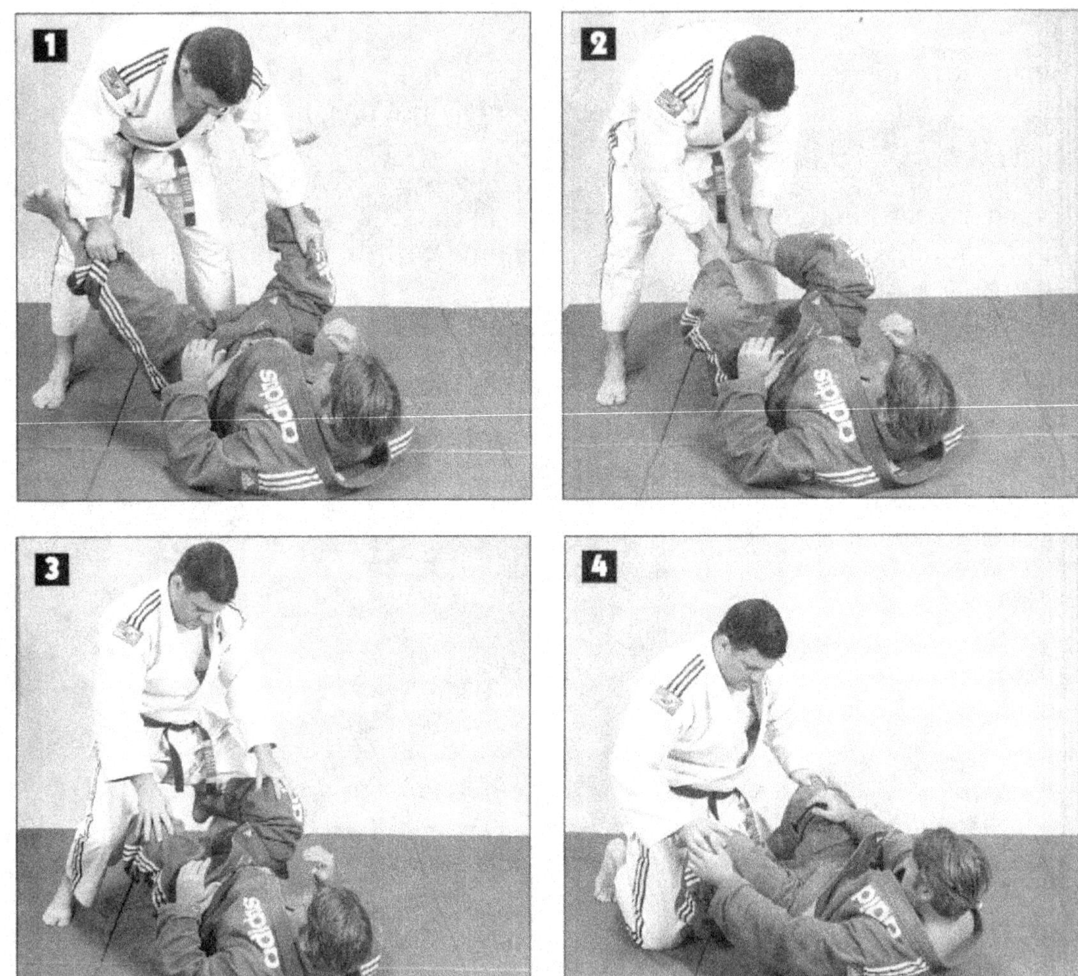

Rigan faces the opponent's open guard (1). He uses his right hand to grab the opponent's left ankle and his left hand to grab the opponent's right ankle (2). Rigan pushes both legs down until they reach the point where he can bring his hips forward (3), and get full control of the opponent's legs (4).

Passing The Guard **30**

He reaches under both legs (5), and grabs the opponent's left pant's leg with his left hand (6). Meanwhile, he maintains a firm grip on the opponent's left knee with his right hand (7). This keeps the opponent's leg still while Rigan passes the guard (8).

continued

continued from page 75

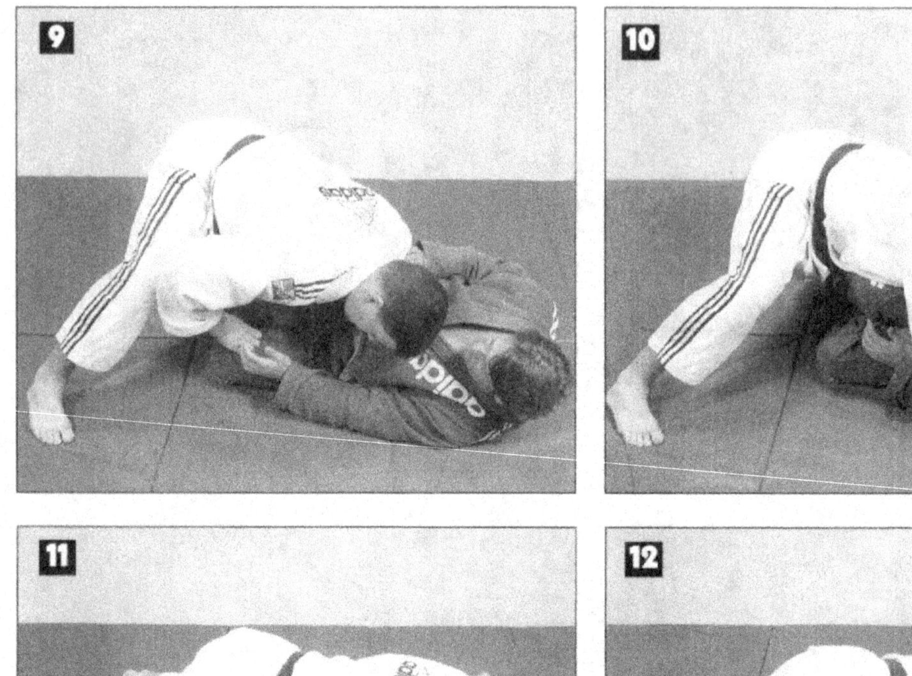

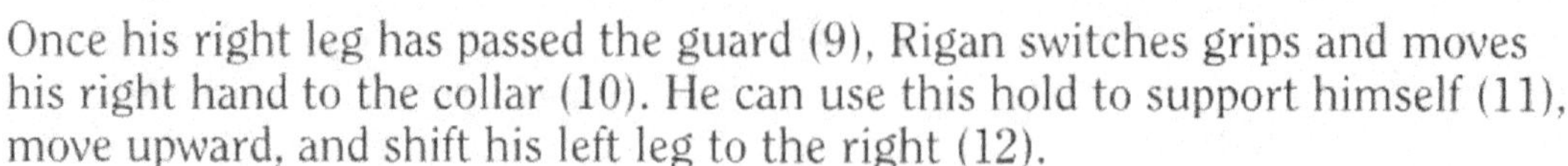

Once his right leg has passed the guard (9), Rigan switches grips and moves his right hand to the collar (10). He can use this hold to support himself (11), move upward, and shift his left leg to the right (12).

Passing The Guard 30

He can now control the opponent's actions (13) before he finally brings his left knee close to the opponent's left hip (14) for full side control (15).

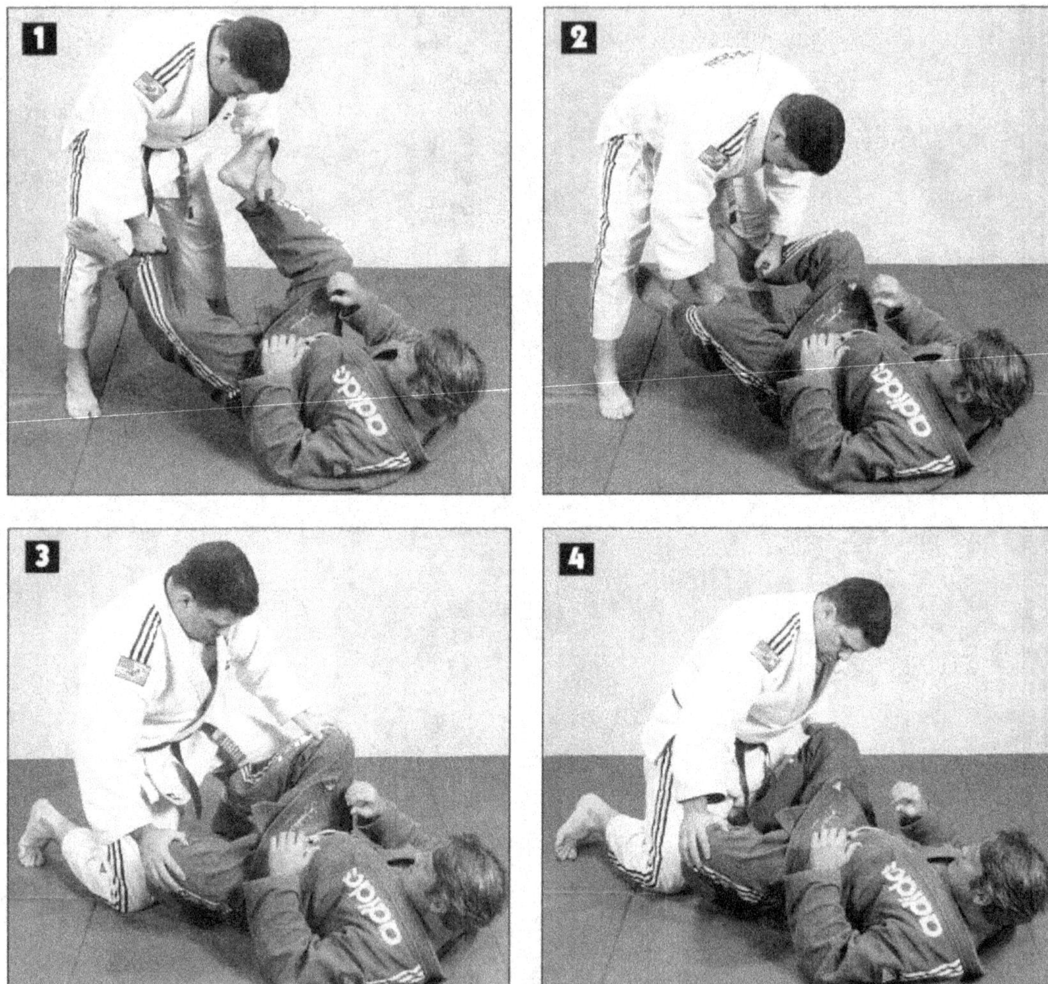

Rigan grabs his opponent's ankles (1), and he pushes them down (2) until they reach the point where he can bring his hips forward (3). This permits him to obtain full control of the opponent's legs (4).

Passing The Guard **31**

He then grabs the legs (5) and latches firmly onto the left pant leg (6). This enables him to pass his right leg to the side (7). Rigan lifts his hips and grabs the opponent's collar (8).

continued

continued from page 79

This gives him momentum (9), and he pushes his body into the air (10-11),

Passing The Guard 31

landing on the opponent's right side (12). Here he assumes the final side control (13).

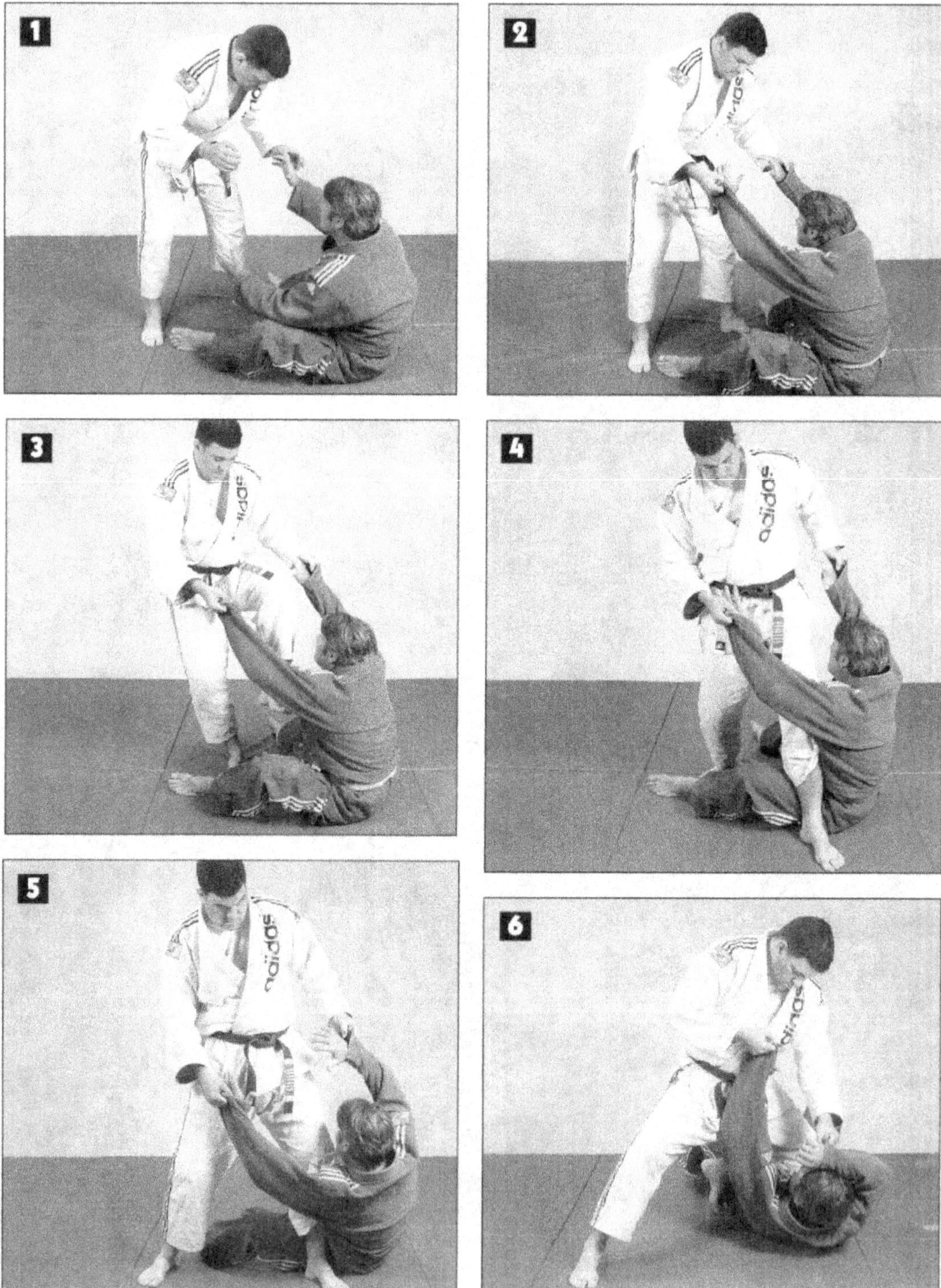

Passing The Guard 32

Rigan faces his opponent (1). He grabs both of the opponent's sleeves (2), steps forward with his left leg (3), and places his leg next to the opponent's left hip (4). By pushing with his hips (5), Rigan forces the opponent to the ground, where he controls him with the knee on his chest (6). While maintaining a tight grip on the opponent's left arm (7), Rigan then grabs the collar (8). This confuses his opponent (9), which gives Rigan the opportunity to submit him with a straight armlock (10).

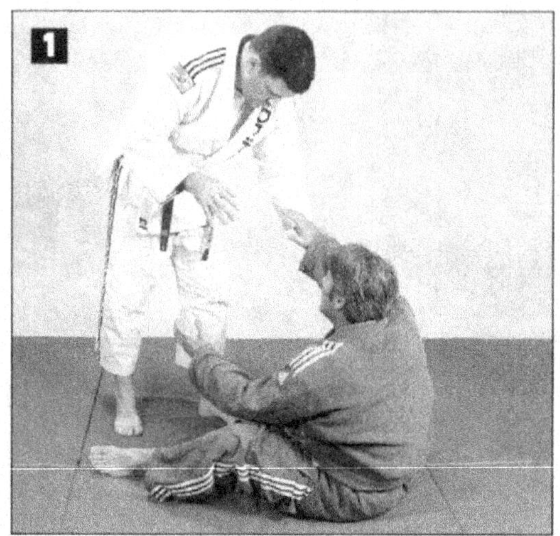

Rigan faces a seated opponent (1). He grabs the opponent's right sleeve with his left hand and uses his right hand to push the opponent's head down (2). This maneuver helps Rigan lift his right leg over (3)

Passing The Guard **33**

the opponent's left shoulder (4). Pushing with his hips forward forces the opponent toward the ground (5-6).

continued

continued from page 85

Before the opponent's back touches the ground, Rigan moves his right leg behind the opponent's neck (7). Rigan rolls to his right (8), bringing

Passing The Guard **33**

the opponent with him. He then reaches his right ankle with his left hand (9), choking his opponent with a *triangle* (10).

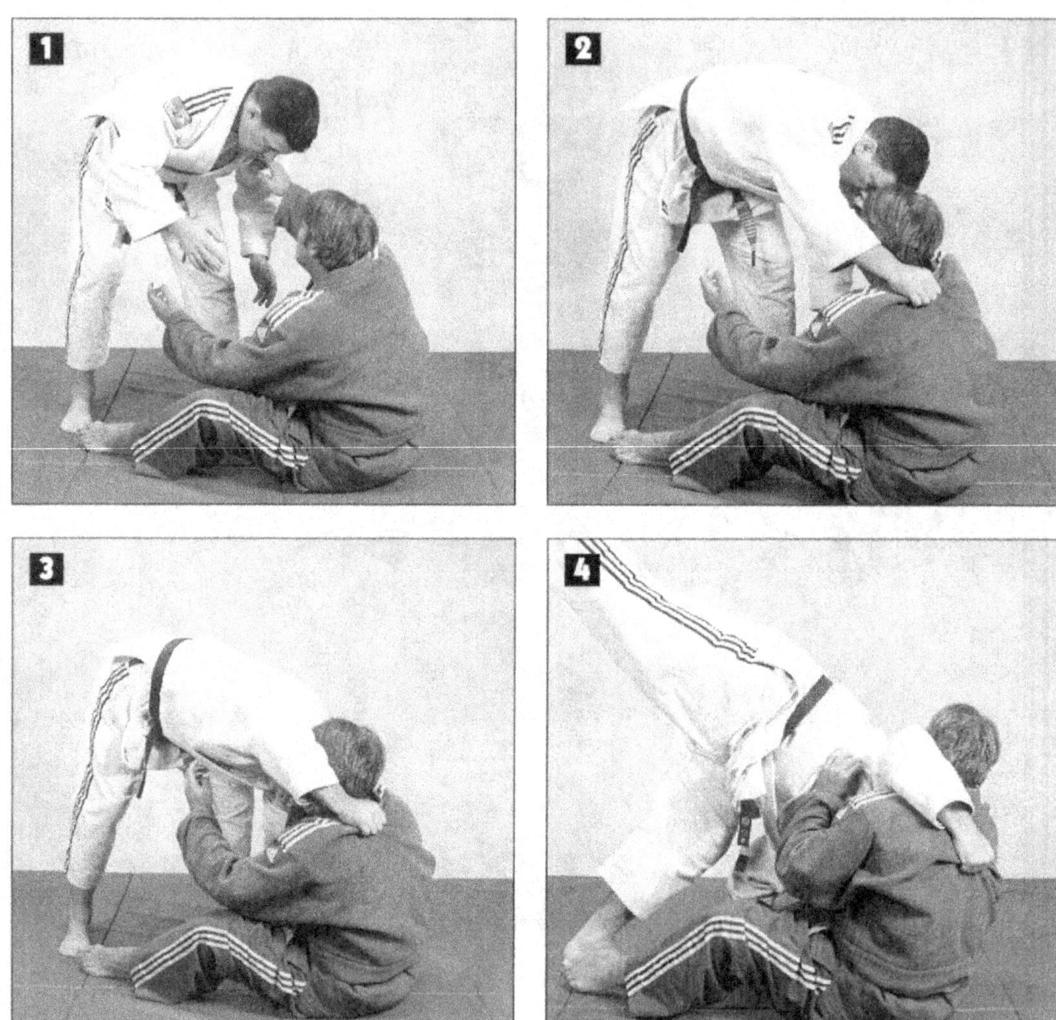

Rigan faces his seated opponent (1), and uses his right hand to grab the back of the opponent's collar (2). Meanwhile, he lowers his left hand to the ground (3), and pushes himself into the air (4-5).

Passing The Guard 34

He lands on the opponent's left (6), and finalizes the move with a side control (7).

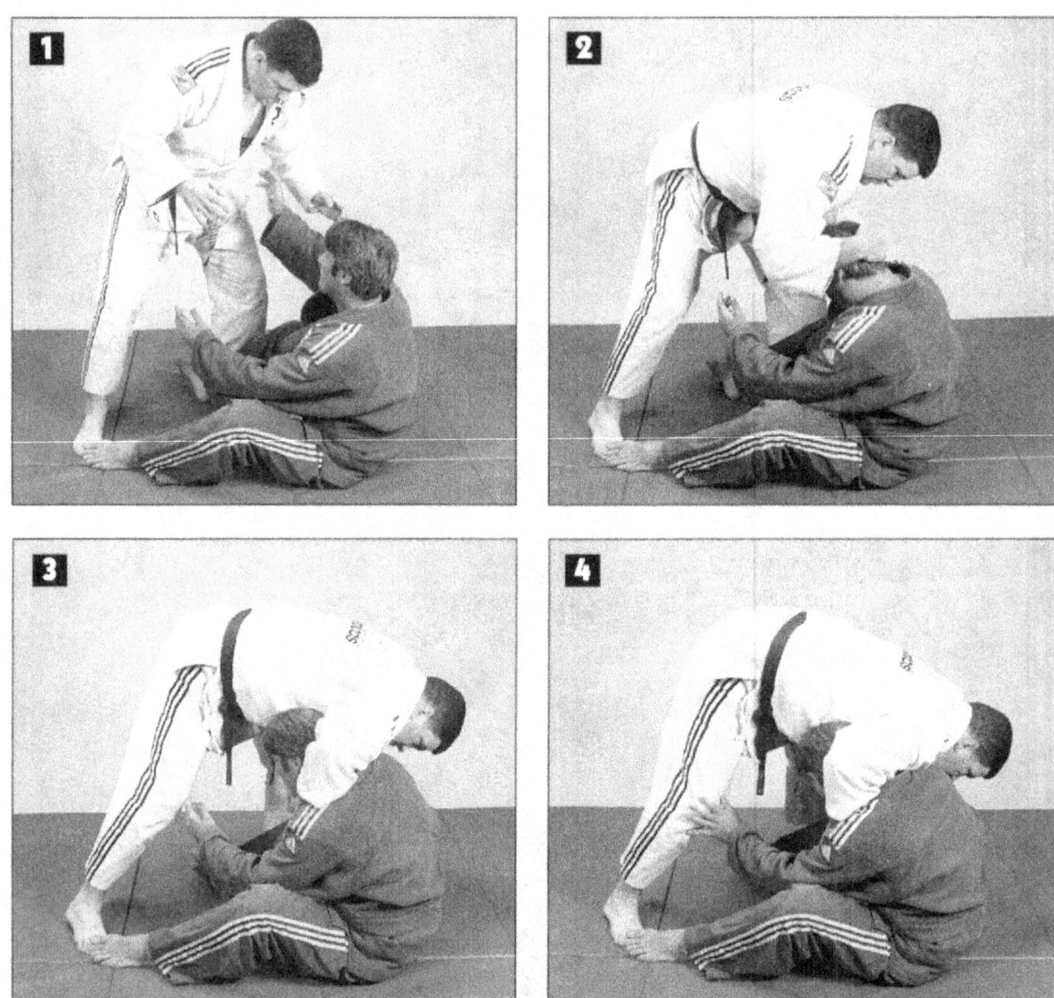

Rigan faces his seated opponent (1). Using his right hand, he grabs the back of the opponent's head (2), and forces him slightly down (3). Rigan slides his arm around the front of the opponent's neck and raises his hips (4).

Passing The Guard 35

This takes his hips out of the opponent's reach (5-6), and prevents the opponent from controlling him. Rigan moves to the right (7), and assumes full side control (8).

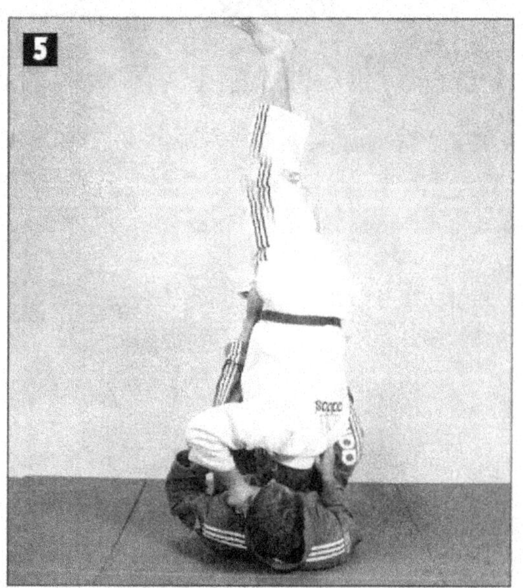

Passing The Guard 36

Rigan starts by grabbing both of the opponent's ankles (1). He first releases the ankle with his left hand and grabs the jacket (2), and then he does the same with his right hand (3). Putting his head onto the opponent's chest (4), Rigan gets momentum to push himself into the air (5-6). He lands on the opponent's left (7), passes the guard (8) and assumes a knee side control (9). To establish that momentum to push yourself into the air, it is important to keep a tight grip and put lots of pressure onto the opponent's chest with your head.

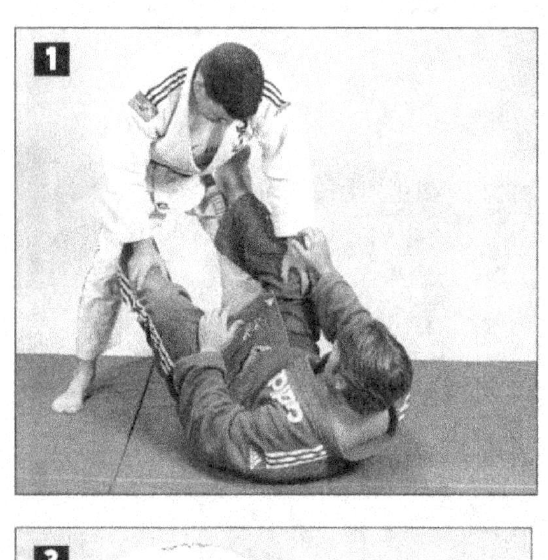

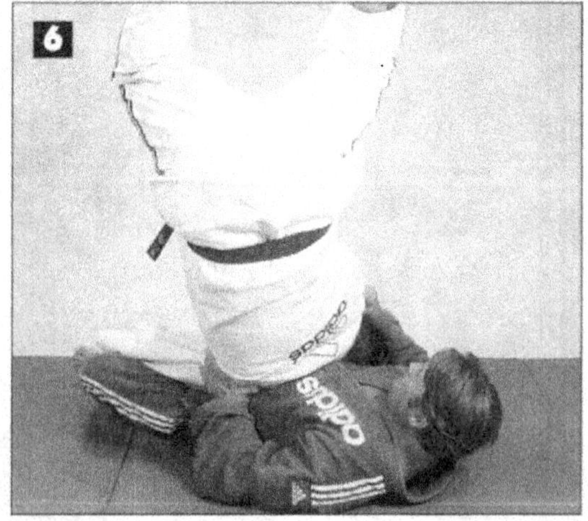

Passing The Guard 37

Rigan faces the opponent's open guard (1). He grabs both ankles (2), and pushes them to the floor (3-4). He puts his head on the opponent's abdomen (5), pushes himself into the air (6) and lands on the other side (7). He immediately starts to roll to the left (8). Using his right hand, Rigan grabs the opponent's collar (9), and then assumes full side control (10).

Rigan faces the opponent's open guard (1). He moves his right leg to the side as he pushes the opponent's left leg down (2). Next, Rigan grabs the opponent's left brankle with his right arm (3), and leans back, bringing his right leg under the opponent's left leg (4).

Passing The Guard 38

Rigan places his left hand over the opponent's left leg, reaches under the opponent's left leg with his right hand, grabs his left wrist and pushes forward with his hips (5). The result is a devastating anklelock (6).

Rigan controls the opponent's left leg with his right arm (1). Rigan lowers his left knee to the opponent's left hip (2), moves to the opponent's left (3), and sits on

Passing The Guard **39**

the floor adjacent to the opponent's left side (4). Note that he still has control of the opponent's left leg. Allowing himself to lean backward to the ground, Rigan pushes his hips forward and applies a kneebar (5).

Using his right arm, Rigan again controls the opponent's left leg (1). Rigan twists his body to the right (2), brings his right leg over the opponent's left hip (3), and prepares to sit (4).

Passing The Guard **40**

Rigan leans all the way back (5), and applies a painful kneebar (6).

Passing The Guard 41

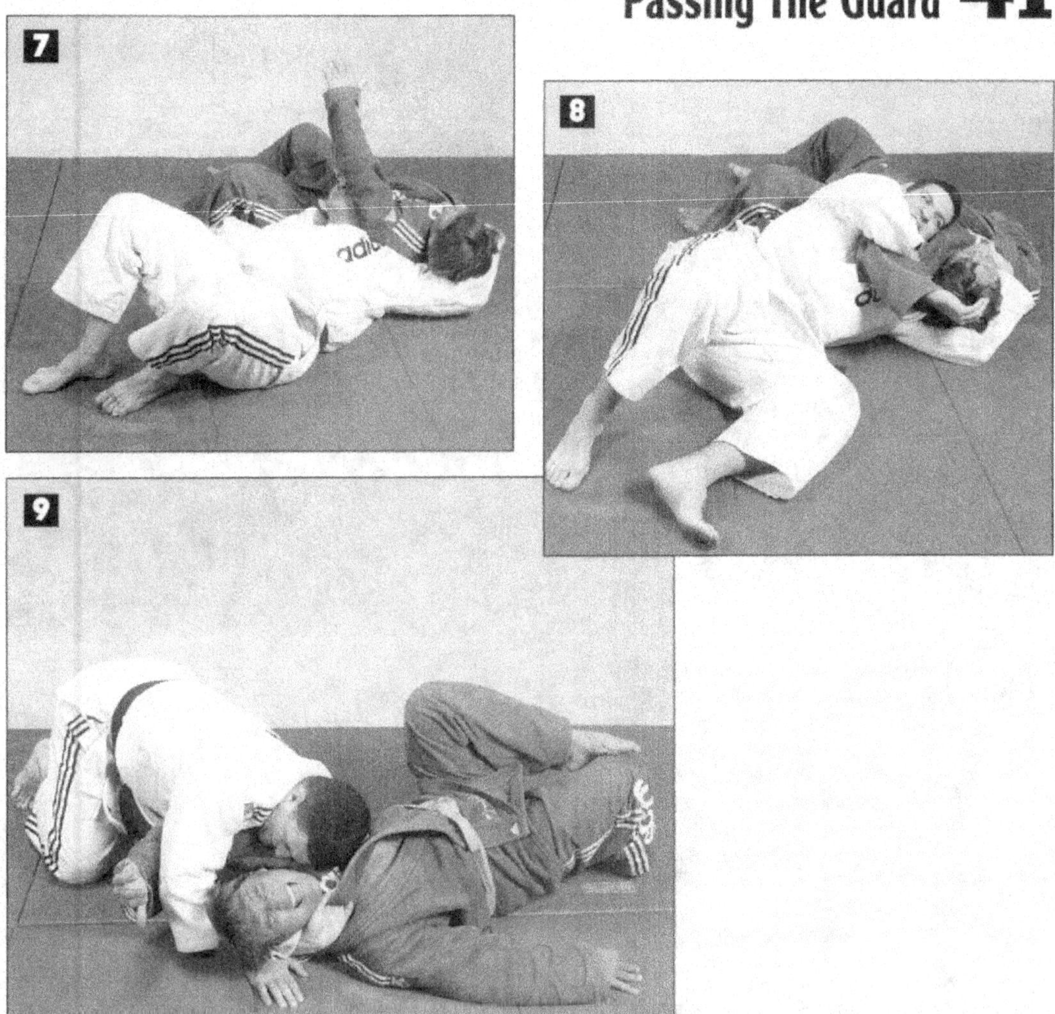

Rigan faces the seated opponent (1). Using his left hand, Rigan grabs the left side of the opponent's collar (2). He brings his left arm around the opponent's neck (3-5), and moves his hips to the right (6). From there, he spins until he's on his back (7). Rigan turns slightly, wraps his right arm around the opponent's left arm, maintains the hold on the opponent's neck (8), and applies a choke (9).

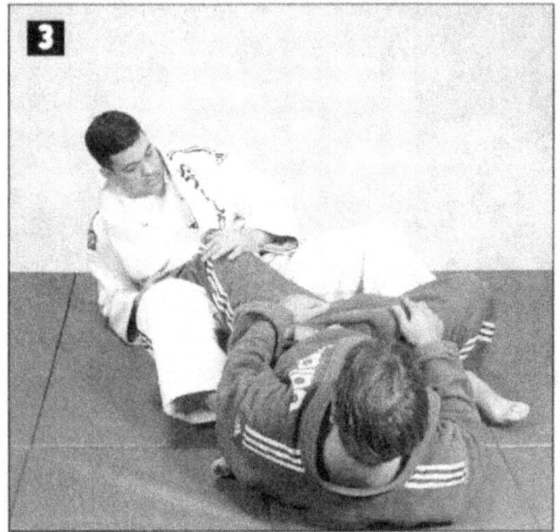

Rigan's opponent places his left leg over Rigan's right hip (1). Rigan pushes the opponent's right leg with his left hand (2), and maintains control of the left leg as he leans backward (3). Once on the ground, Rigan passes his right leg over the opponent's left leg (4-5).

Passing The Guard **42**

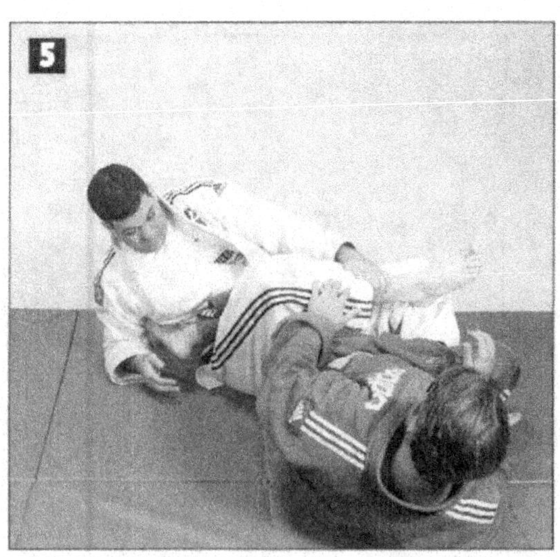

Rigan hooks his right instep under
his left leg (6), joins his hands, cranks the opponent's ankle and applies the
painful lock (7-8).

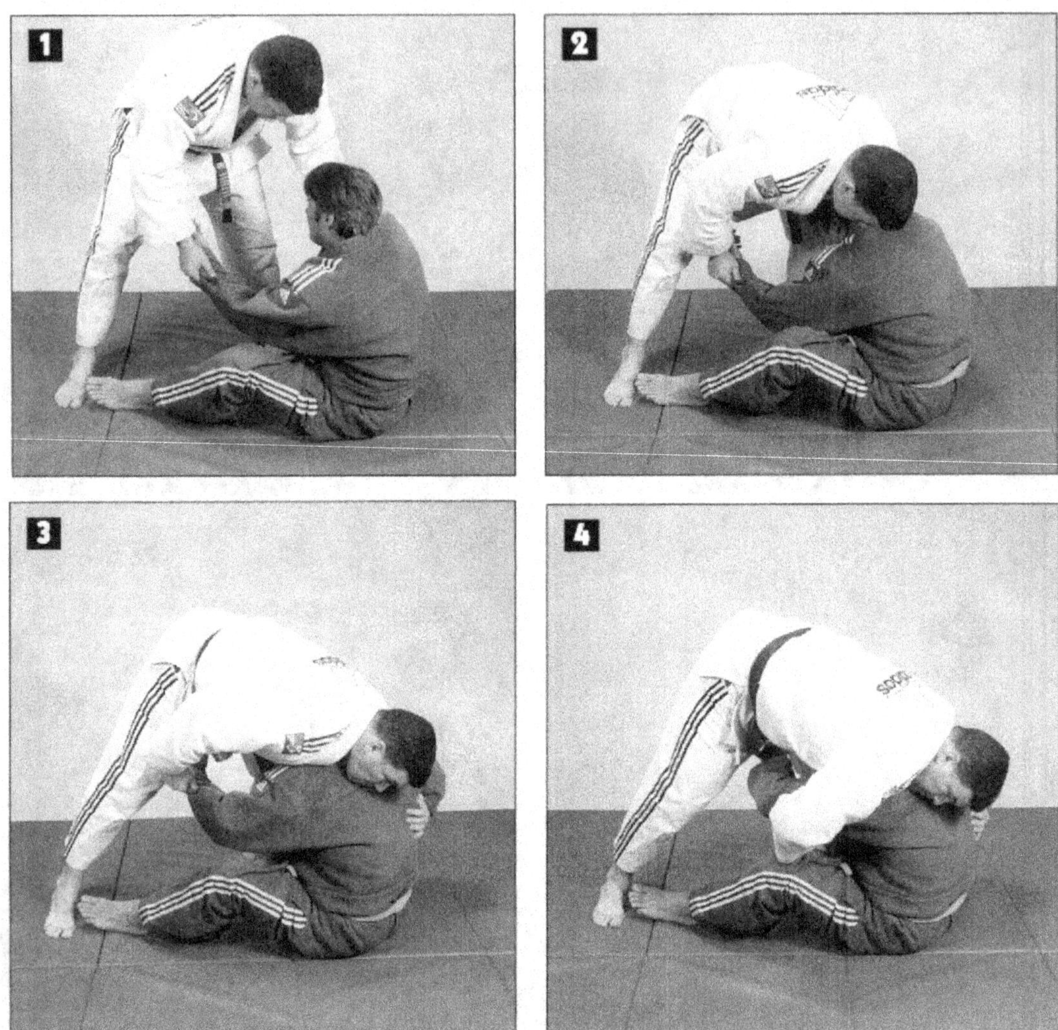

Rigan faces the opponent (1). He leans forward (2), and places his left hand under the opponent's right armpit as he maintains a safe distance by keeping his hips away (3). Rigan uses his right hand to control the opponent's left arm (4).

Passing The Guard **43**

The opponent cannot stop Rigan from passing his right leg to the left side (5). Rigan can now finalize the move by taking the opponent to his back and controlling him from the side (6).

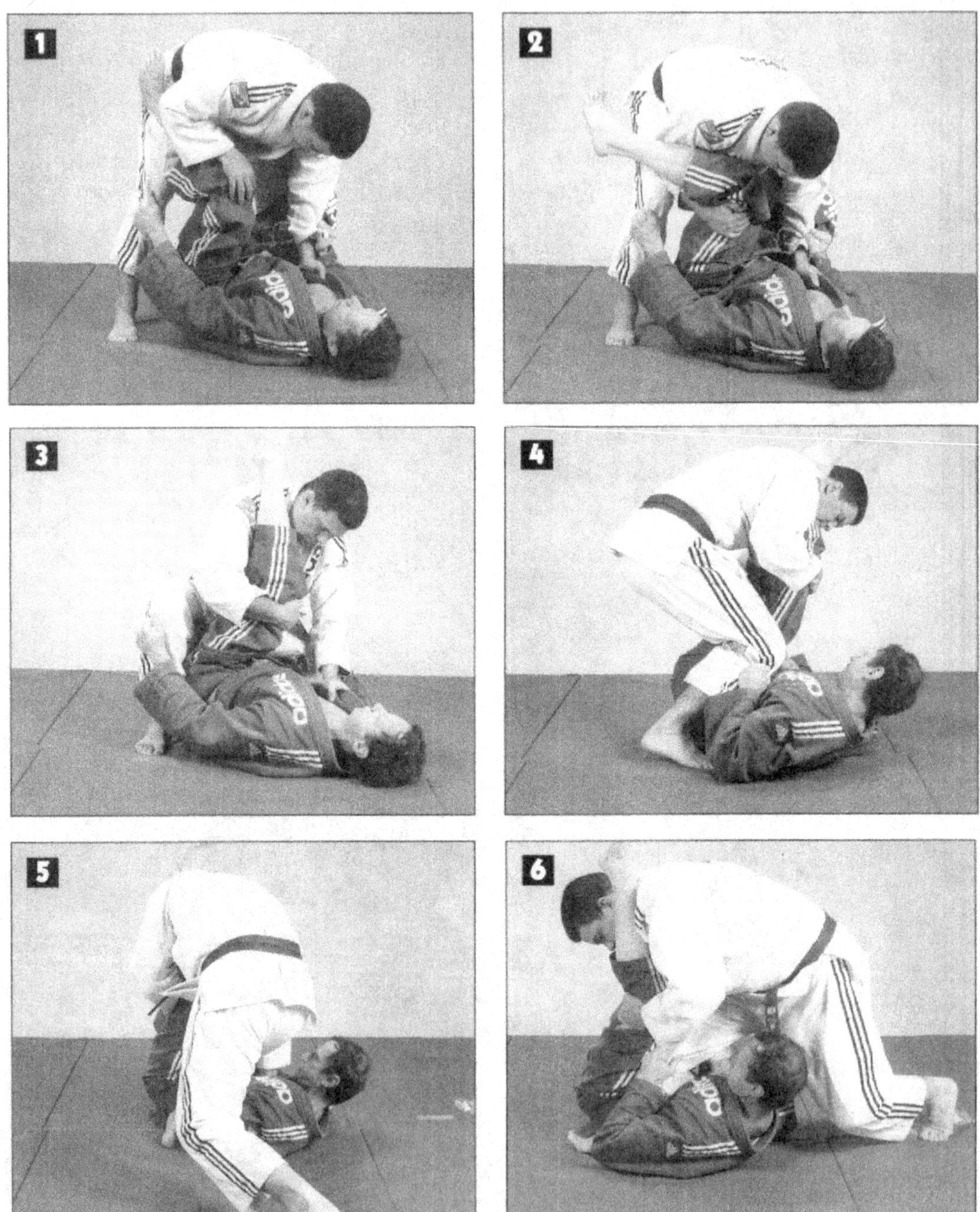

Passing The Guard 44

Rigan initiates the passing of the guard (1) by moving his right arm under the opponent's left leg. Next, he lowers his hips to keep the center of gravity low (2-3). Using his right knee as pivot point (4), Rigan moves his left leg around (5), and ultimately brings it to the other side (6). Rigan releases the opponent's left leg and controls him from the mount position (7).

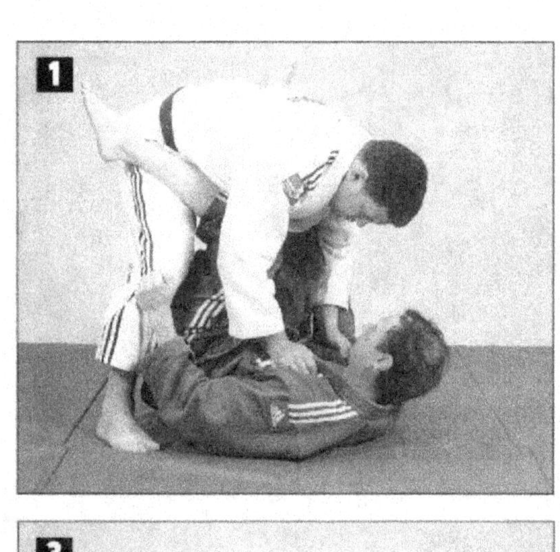

Passing The Guard 45

Rigan tries to pass the opponent's guard (1), but he is countered with a sweeping technique. Rigan prevents himself from falling by placing both hands on the ground (2-3), and he immediately turns to his right (4). He controls the opponent's body (5), close and tight (6). He assumes side control, where he can now initiate the counterattack (7).

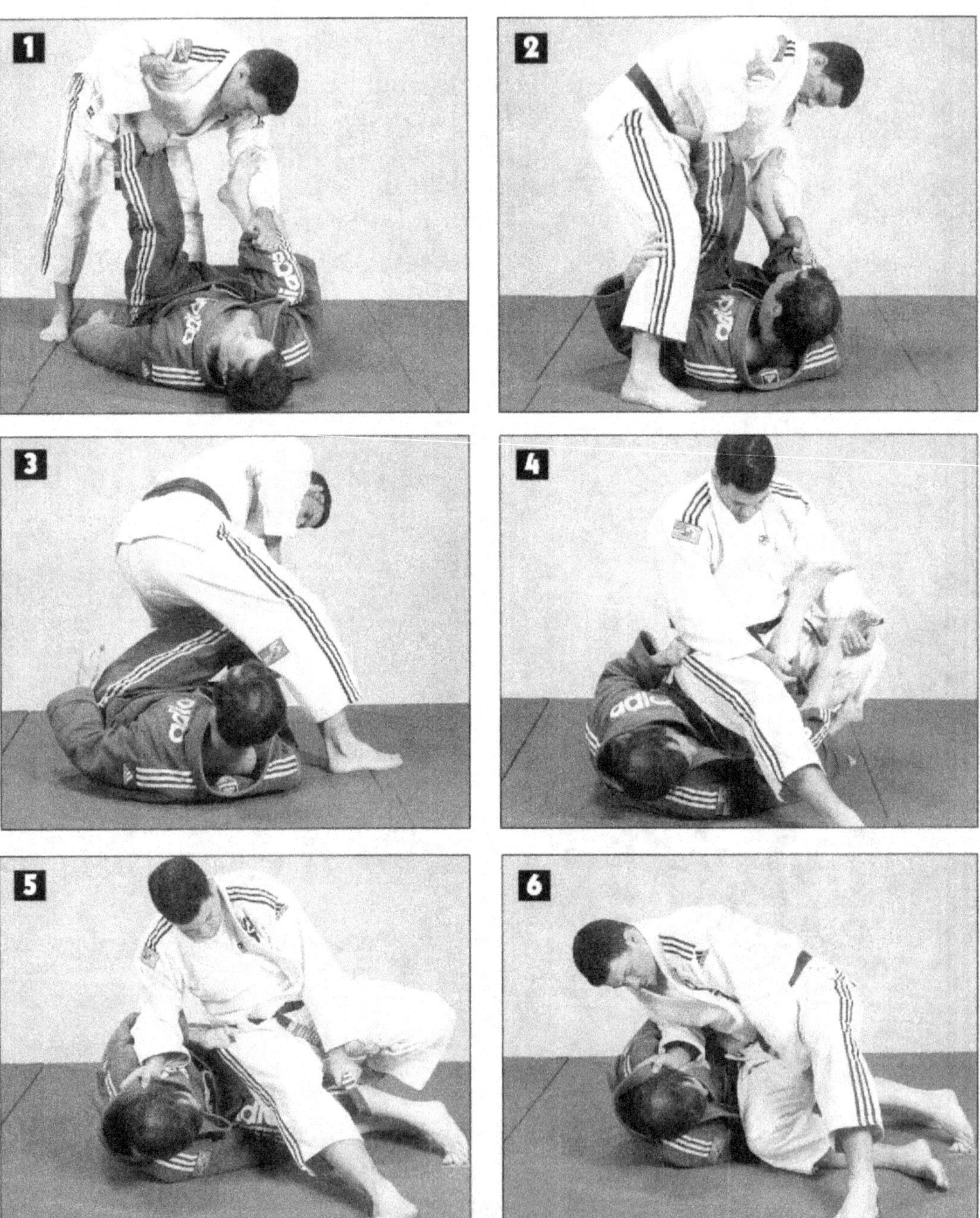

Passing The Guard 46

Rigan tries to pass the opponent's open guard (1). He moves his right leg to the side as he pulls the opponent's left leg (2). This allows him to move his right leg to the other side (3). Having full control of both of the opponent's legs, Rigan sits (4) and slides to the left (5). While doing this, he uses his right hand to control one side of the opponent's collar (6), and his left hand to grab the other side of the collar (7). Finally, he applies pressure from the side (8).

Rigan tries to pass the open guard (1), but the opponent maintains tight control of his movements, which forces Rigan to place his left knee on the opponent's chest (2).

Passing The Guard 47

Rigan now focuses on getting a submission by controlling the opponent's left foot (3). Ultimately, he applies an anklelock (4).

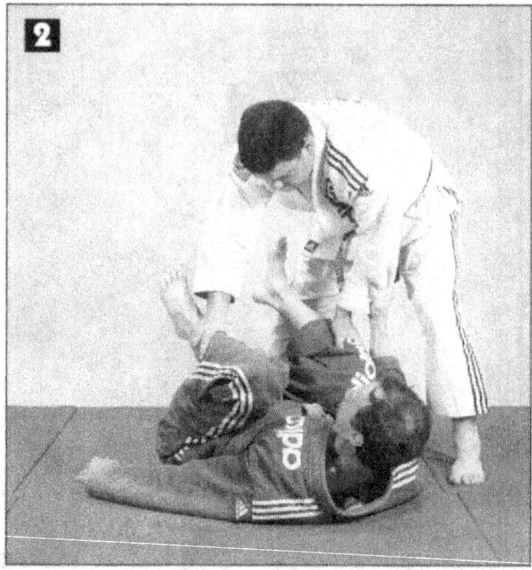

Rigan faces his opponent's open guard (1). As he controls both of the opponent's legs, Rigan circles to the left (2). Using his right hand, he grabs his opponent's left ankle (3). He lowers his left knee onto the chest (4).

Passing The Guard 48

Rigan rolls over the opponent (5), and applies an anklelock (6).

Rigan is in the opponent's closed guard (1). He lowers his body (2), passes his left hand behind the opponent's neck (3), and grabs his own sleeve (4).

Passing The Guard 49

He raises the edge of his right forearm to the front of the opponent's neck (5), and chokes him with an *ezequiel* (6).

Rigan is inside the opponent's closed guard (1). Rigan grabs the opponent's left wrist (2), lifts his hips and "walks" forward (3-4).

Passing The Guard 50

Notice the space between the opponent's back and the floor. Rigan passes the opponent's left wrist under the upraised back (5), and grabs the arm on the other side (6).

continued

continued from page 121

Rigan uses his right hand to push the opponent's left knee down (7-8).

Note: As you "walk" forward in the beginning of the technique, remember to keep strong pressure on the opponent's body. It is also important to make sure the opponent's arm gets trapped between his back and the floor as you move to the side. When his hands are trapped, it will be impossible for him to prevent you from passing the guard.

Passing The Guard **50**

This enables him to pass his right leg (9) and then his body over the opponent (10). Now he can obtain side control and initiate the attack (11).

Rigan is in the opponent's closed guard (1). He reaches the back of the opponent's neck with his right hand (2), and then his left hand (3).

Passing The Guard 51

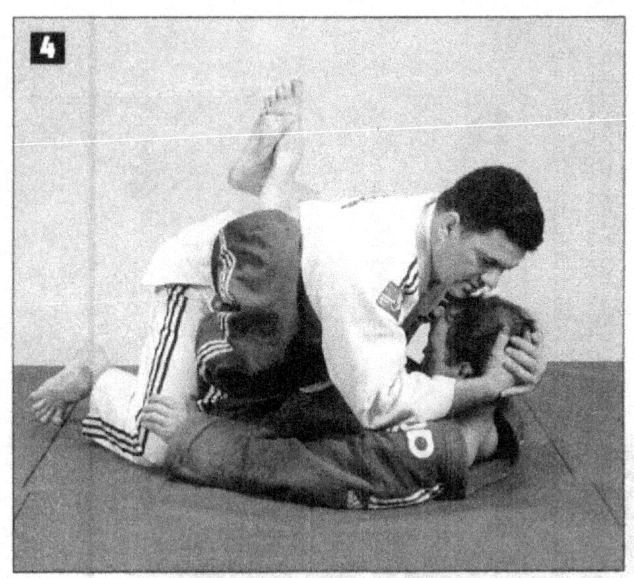

Keeping his elbows close and tight to the opponent's body (4), Rigan applies pressure and executes a neck crunch to submit him (5).

Passing The Guard **52**

Rigan is inside the opponent's guard (1). He brings his right leg up and grabs the opponent's gi (2). Rigan quickly rips the uniform off his opponent's shoulder, trapping the left arm (3-4). He reinforces the hold by grabbing the jacket with his left hand, which is under the opponent's back (5-6).

continued

continued from page 127

Once the arm has been trapped, Rigan uses his right hand (7), to push the opponent's left knee down (8-9). He passes his right knee over his opponent (10),

Passing The Guard 52

and then his entire body (11). Now he can start an offensive action (12).

Rigan tries to pass the guard (1), but his opponent counters with a sweeping technique.

Passing The Guard 53

Rigan prevents himself from falling with both hands (2-3), immediately turns to his right, controls the opponent's right leg close and tight, and executes a reverse anklelock (4).

Rigan tries to pass the opponent's guard from the left side (1). As he feels the opponent controlling the situation, Rigan grabs the left leg with his left hand (2), pushes the opponent's hips to the left and "walks" to the right (3).

Passing The Guard 54

With his right hand, Rigan reaches around the back of the opponent's neck and grabs the collar (4). He shifts over and assumes side control (5).

Rigan tries to pass the opponent's guard (1). Using his left leg, the opponent blocks Rigan's move and slides his hips to the right (2-3). Rigan counters by controlling the opponent's belt (4), raising his hips (5), and pulling the

Passing The Guard 55

opponent's right leg and right arm
(6). Rigan then releases the leg (7),
and gains better control of the
right arm before going for the
armlock (8).

Rigan tries to pass the guard (1), but
the opponent prevents him from
doing this by placing his foot on
Rigan's right hip. Rigan grabs the
collar of his own gi with his left hand
(2), and uses his right hand to grab
the opponent's left wrist (3). With his
opponent's right leg still up, Rigan
starts "walking" forward (4).

Passing The Guard 56

This puts pressure on the opponent. Rigan circles to the right, avoiding contact with the opponent's hips (5). Rigan immediately leans backwards and places his left knee at the opponent's left armpit (6). He slightly moves his hips to the right (7), and applies a finishing armlock (8).

Rigan begins inside the opponent's guard (1). He then moves his hips back to create space (2), which enables him to move his left knee to the opponent's coccyx (3).

Passing The Guard 57

With both hands firmly on the opponent's belt, Rigan applies pressure and increases the space between them (4). He then immediately brings his left knee up to start the offensive action (5).

Passing The Guard 58

Rigan is inside the opponent's guard (1). He grabs the opponent's jacket with his right hand (2), applying pressure to the left armpit. He does the same thing with his left hand and leans forward (3-4). Maintaining pressure with his hips, Rigan "walks" forward until his opponent's hips are off the ground (5).

He then brings his left knee forward to the middle of the opponent's lower back or coccyx (6), and starts to sit (7). The pressure on the opponent's lower back forces him to open his legs (8). This allows Rigan to bring his left knee up so he can begin passing the guard (9).

Rigan is inside the opponent's closed guard (1). While holding onto the opponent's gi, Rigan straightens his trunk (2), and initiates the offensive (3) by bringing his left leg up (4). He then does the same thing with the right leg (5).

Passing The Guard 59

Without releasing his grip on the opponent's gi, Rigan stands (6), and uses his right hand to push the opponent's left knee down (7). This opens the guard (8).

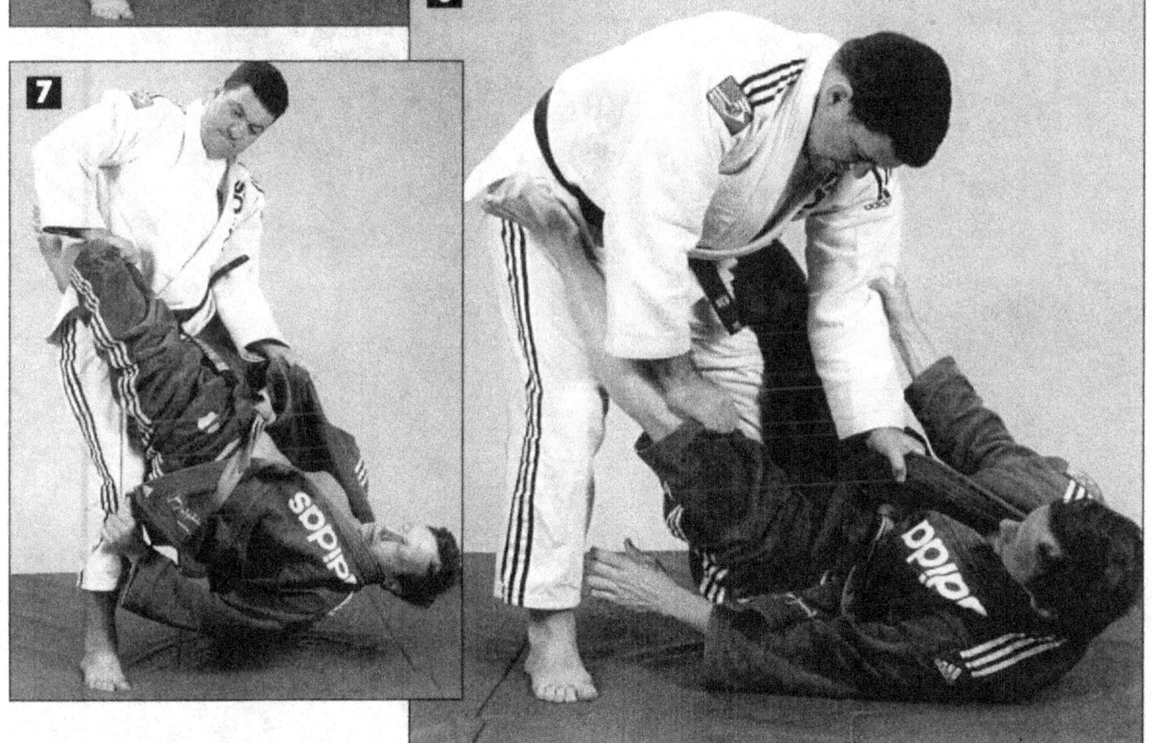

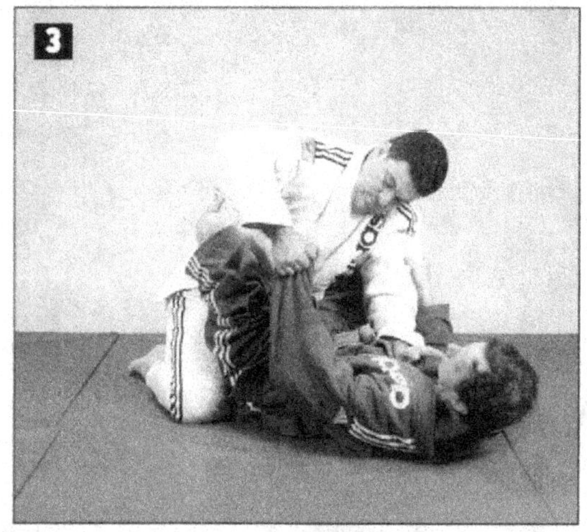

Passing The Guard 60

Rigan begins inside the opponent's guard (1). Using his right hand, Rigan grabs the opponent's left sleeve (2-3), and forces the opponent's arm over the stomach (4). Rigan maintains control with the left hand (5), and begins to stand (6). Once he is up (7), Rigan uses his left hand to push the opponent's right knee down (8) to open the guard (9).

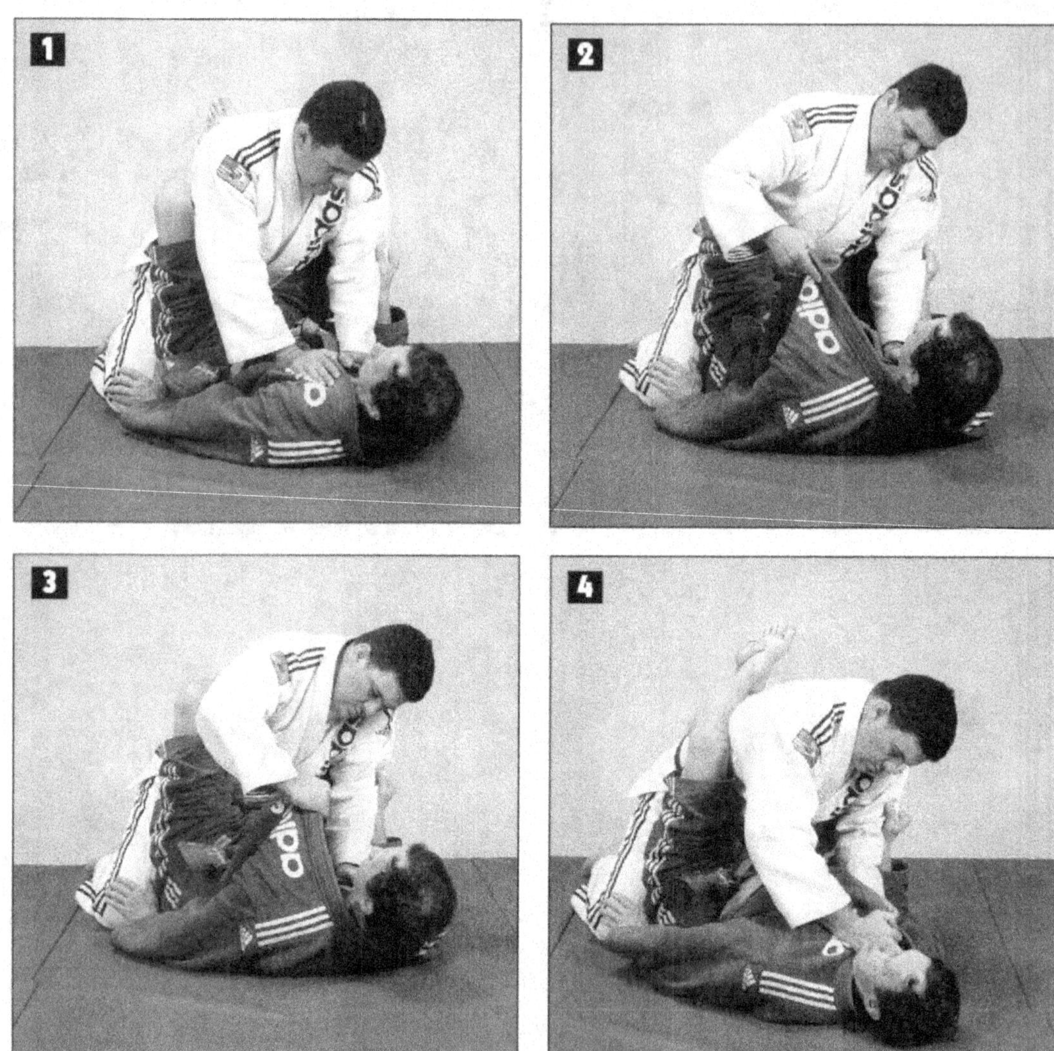

Rigan begins inside the opponent's guard (1). Using his right hand, Rigan grabs the gi (2), and moves it across the opponent's neck (3-4).

Passing The Guard **61**

He uses his left hand to grab the other side of the collar (5). By pulling with his left hand and pushing with his right, Rigan chokes his opponent (6).

Keeping both hands inside, Rigan tries to pass the opponent's open guard (1). He squats and uses his left knee to put pressure on the opponent's right thigh (2).

Passing The Guard 62

When he reaches the ground (3), Rigan moves to the side, uses his right knee to block the opponent's attempt to put him back into the guard and assumes side control (4).

While keeping both hands inside, Rigan tries to pass the opponent's open guard (1). He lowers his body and uses his left knee to put pressure on the opponent's right thigh (2). Now that he's even lower, Rigan can reach around to the back of the opponent's collar (3).

Passing The Guard 63

Rigan rolls across the opponent and grabs the fighter's left wrist with his right hand (4). He lifts the opponent's arm (5), slides his left arm under (6), and applies a painful *kimura* (7).

SIDE CONTROL

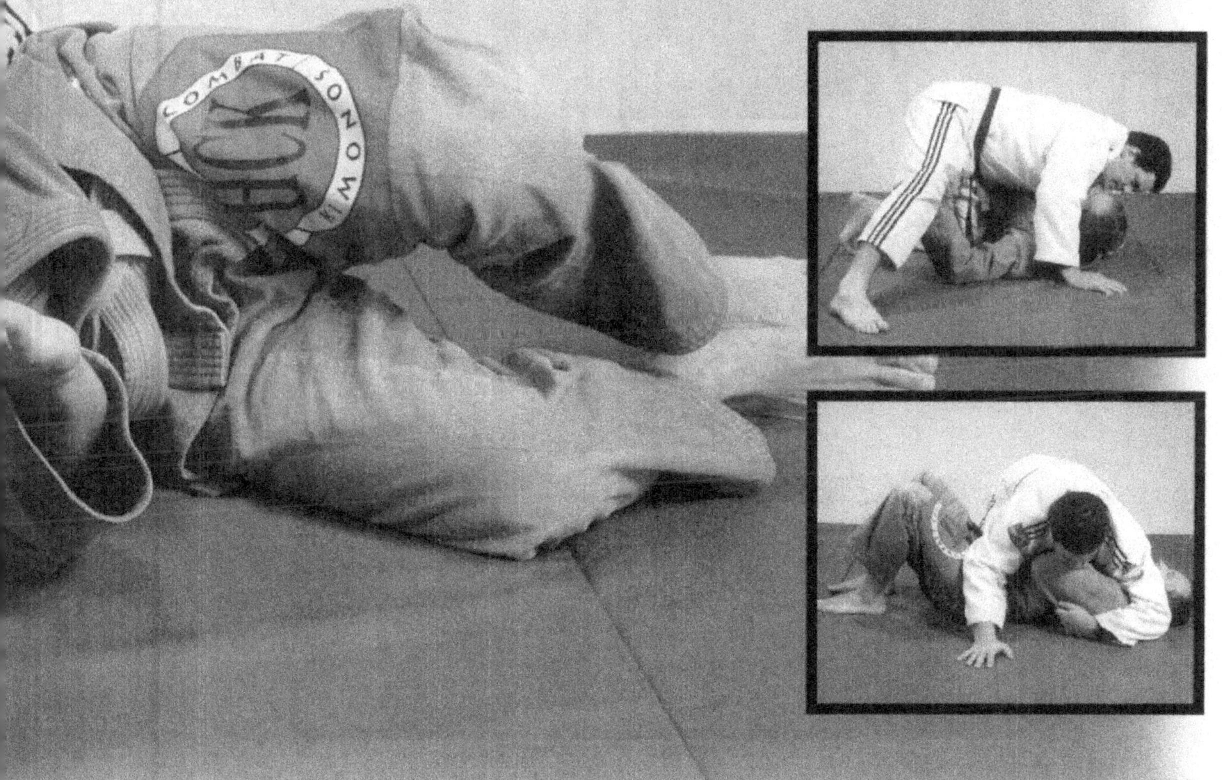

Side Control **1**

Rigan controls his opponent from the side (1). He uses his right hand to grab the opponent's collar and his left hand to grab the belt (2). Rigan starts to stand and places his left knee on the opponent's stomach (3).

Immediately, he switches grips and moves his right hand to the opponent's left sleeve and his left to the left side of the collar (4). Rigan pushes the opponent's left arm to the opposite side (5), and moves his right leg over the opponent's head (6). Keeping tight control over the left arm, Rigan leans back (7), and applies a straight armlock (8). During the whole movement, it is important to keep a tight grip on the opponent's arm and make sure your left knee stays close to his left armpit.

Rigan controls the opponent from the side (1). Then he uses his right arm to trap the opponent's right arm (2). Keeping a tight grip on that arm, Rigan circles around the other side (3-4), leans back (5), and finishes

Side Control **2**

his opponent off with an armlock (6).

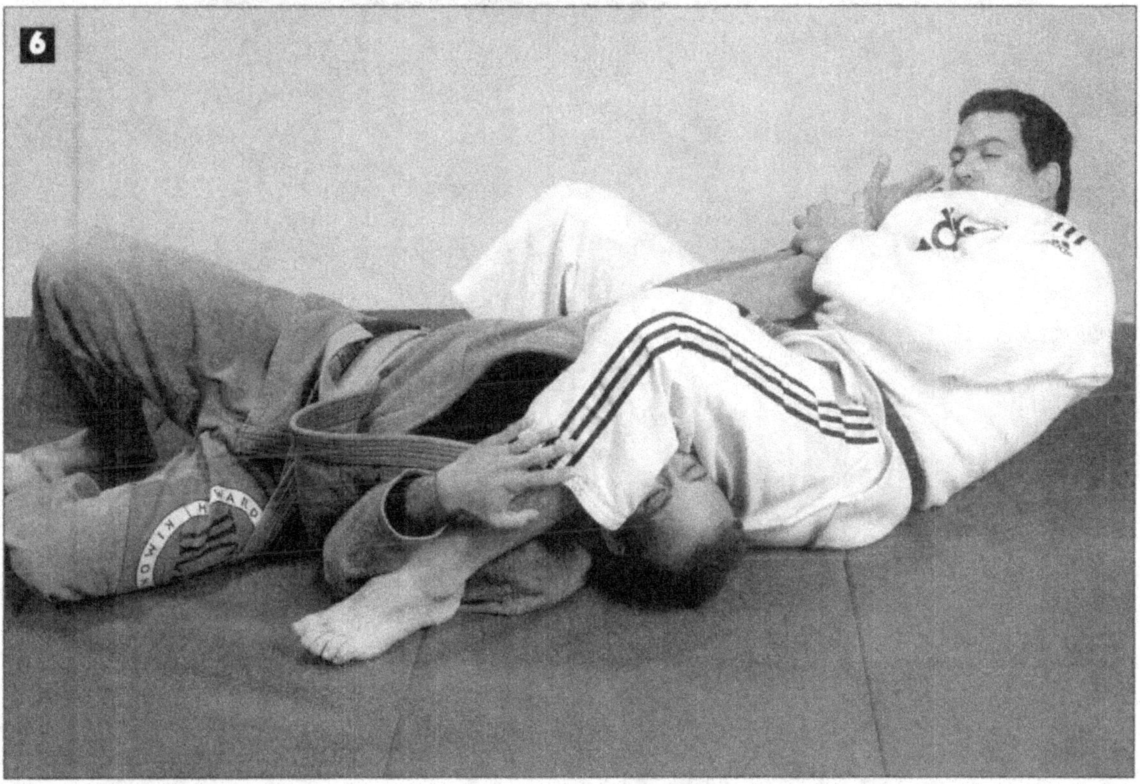

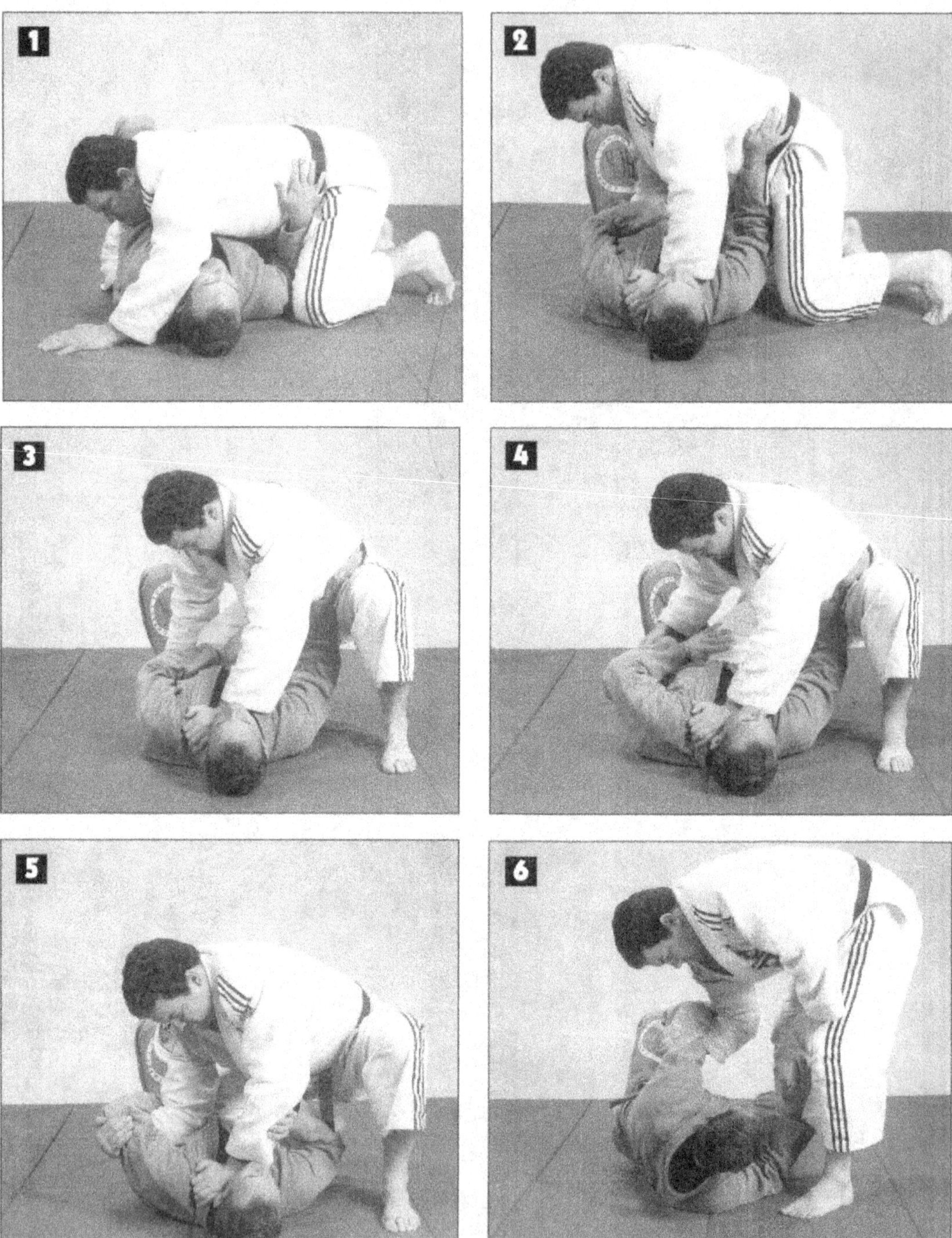

Side Control 3

While controlling the opponent from the side (1), Rigan pushes himself up
(2). Next, he puts his right knee on the opponent's chest (3) as he grabs the
left arm (4). He passes his right arm under the opponent's left arm (5), stands
and circles around (6-7) until he reaches the other side. He sits (8) and
applies a finishing armlock (9).

The opponent reacts to Rigan's side control by turning his body away (1). Using his left hand, Rigan loosens the opponent's gi (2).

Side Control 4

Using his right hand, Rigan reaches around the opponent's neck and grabs the jacket (3). To apply the finishing choke, Rigan tightens the grip with his right hand and puts his left hand over the opposite side of the opponent's neck (4).

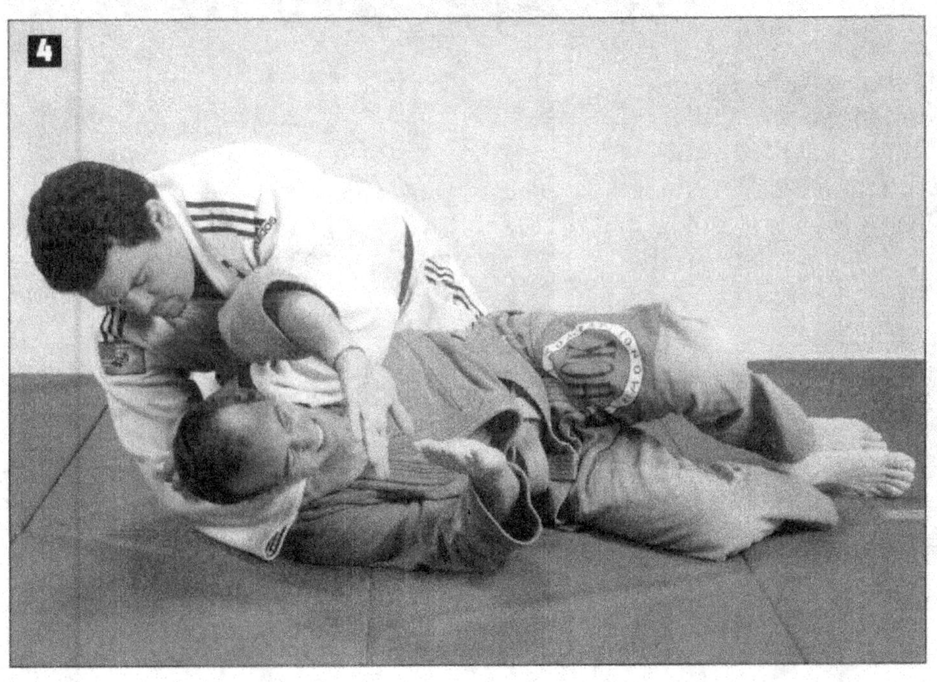

Rigan establishes side control over his opponent (1). While maintaining contact with the adversary, Rigan switches the position of his hips (2), and then grabs the opponent's right wrist (3).

Side Control 5

He switches his hips again, passes his left hand under the opponent's arm (4), and applies a bent armlock (5).

Rigan partially controls the opponent from the side (1). To prevent Rigan from gaining full control, the opponent pushes Rigan's right knee (2). Rigan uses his right hand to grab the opponent's left arm (3).

Side Control 6

He pulls the arm up, switches his hips and adopts a side control with his left arm under the opponent's head (4). He grabs the trapped arm with his right hand (5), and forces it down (6), trapping it with his left leg (7). Rigan grabs his left hand and pulls back, subjecting his opponent to a painful neck crank (8).

Rigan controls the opponent from the side (1). When the opponent tries to stop Rigan's right knee, Rigan pulls the opponent's arm up (2), and switches his hips for better position (3). He can now control the opponent's left arm (4).

Side Control **7**

Rigan passes his left arm under the opponent's head and grabs his own leg just inside the knee (5). Next, he leans forward and grabs his left wrist (6). Pulling back, Rigan applies a neck crank (7).

Rigan establishes control from the side (1), but the opponent keeps pushing Rigan's right knee to prevent full control. Using his right hand, Rigan grabs the opponent's arm (2). While pulling the arm up, Rigan switches his hips (3), and adopts side control with his left arm under the opponent's head (4).

Side Control 8

Notice that Rigan is grabbing his left leg just inside the knee. Next, Rigan controls the opponent's left leg with his right hand (5). For better control, Rigan also grabs his right thigh (6). Rigan applies pressure and executes a painful crank to his opponent's body and neck (7).

Rigan maintains control from the side, but the opponent uses his right knee to prevent Rigan from mounting him (1). Rigan moves his right hand over the opponent's right shin, which forces the right foot forward (2). Using his left hand (3), Rigan grabs

Side Control **9**

the opponent's instep (4). He then reaches under with his right hand and applies an anklelock (5).

Rigan establishes control from the side, but the opponent uses his right knee to prevent Rigan from mounting him (1). Rigan moves his hips back slightly (2), and grabs the opponent's right calf (3).

Side Control **10**

He moves his hips forward, slides his left knee onto the opponent's pelvis (4), leans back and applies a painful kneebar (5).

Rigan maintains control from the side, but the opponent again uses his right knee to prevent Rigan from mounting him (1). This time Rigan changes his strategy. First, using both hands, he grabs the opponent's left arm (2). This forces the opponent to roll to the opposite side to avoid the control (3). Rigan then brings his left leg over the opponent's head (4).

Side Control 11

When the opponent tries to use his right hand to release Rigan's grip (5), Rigan switches the grip and grabs the opponent's right arm as he simultaneously sits (6) to apply a finishing armlock (7).

Controlling the altercation from the side (1), Rigan pushes his body up (2), and puts his right knee on the opponent's chest (3). Notice that he maintains his left hand on the opponent's collar. With the palm up (4), Rigan slides

Side Control **12**

his right hand under his left (5), and applies a front choke (6).

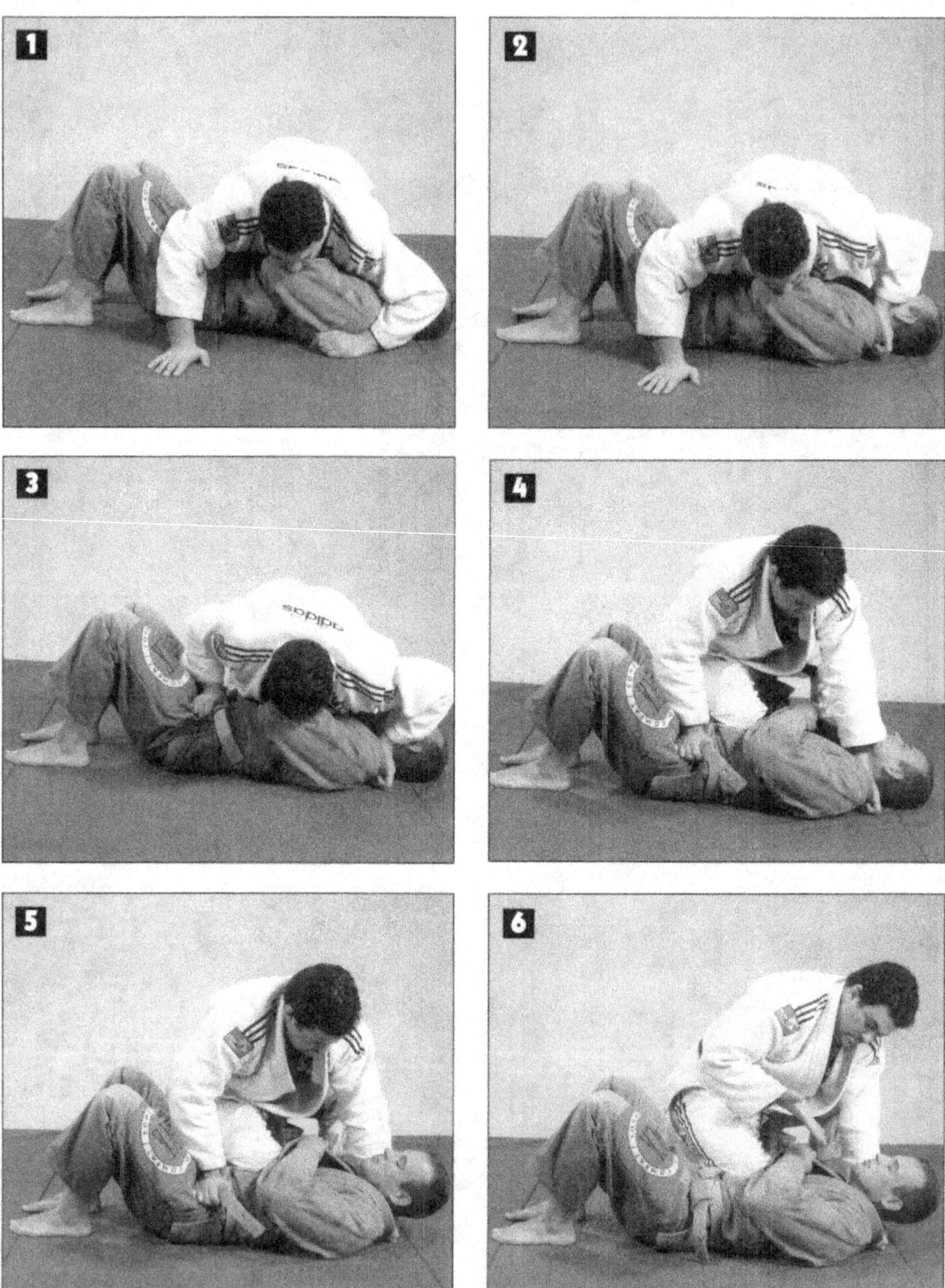

Side Control 13

Rigan controls the opponent from the side (1). He puts his left hand on the opponent's collar (2) and his right hand on the opponent's belt (3). He raises himself and puts his right knee on the opponent's chest (4). While maintaining his grip on the collar, he moves his hand to the other side of the neck (5). Rigan places his right hand exactly where his left hand was (6-7). Without releasing his grip, Rigan circles around the opponent's head (8).

This enables him to make the grip even tighter. By leaning forward, Rigan creates additional pressure and executes a finishing choke (9).

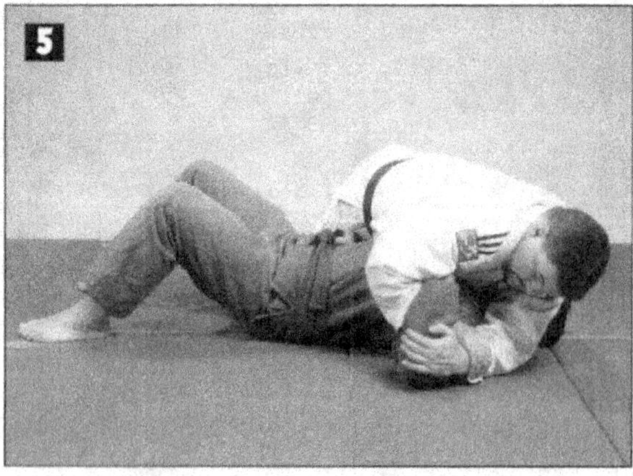

Rigan establishes control from the side, but the opponent is grabbing his own belt, which prevents Rigan from getting an armlock (1). Rigan slides his right arm under the opponent's left arm (2), and latches onto the triceps (3). He uses his left arm to grab the opponent's elbow, forming a "Figure 4" lock (4).

Side Control 14

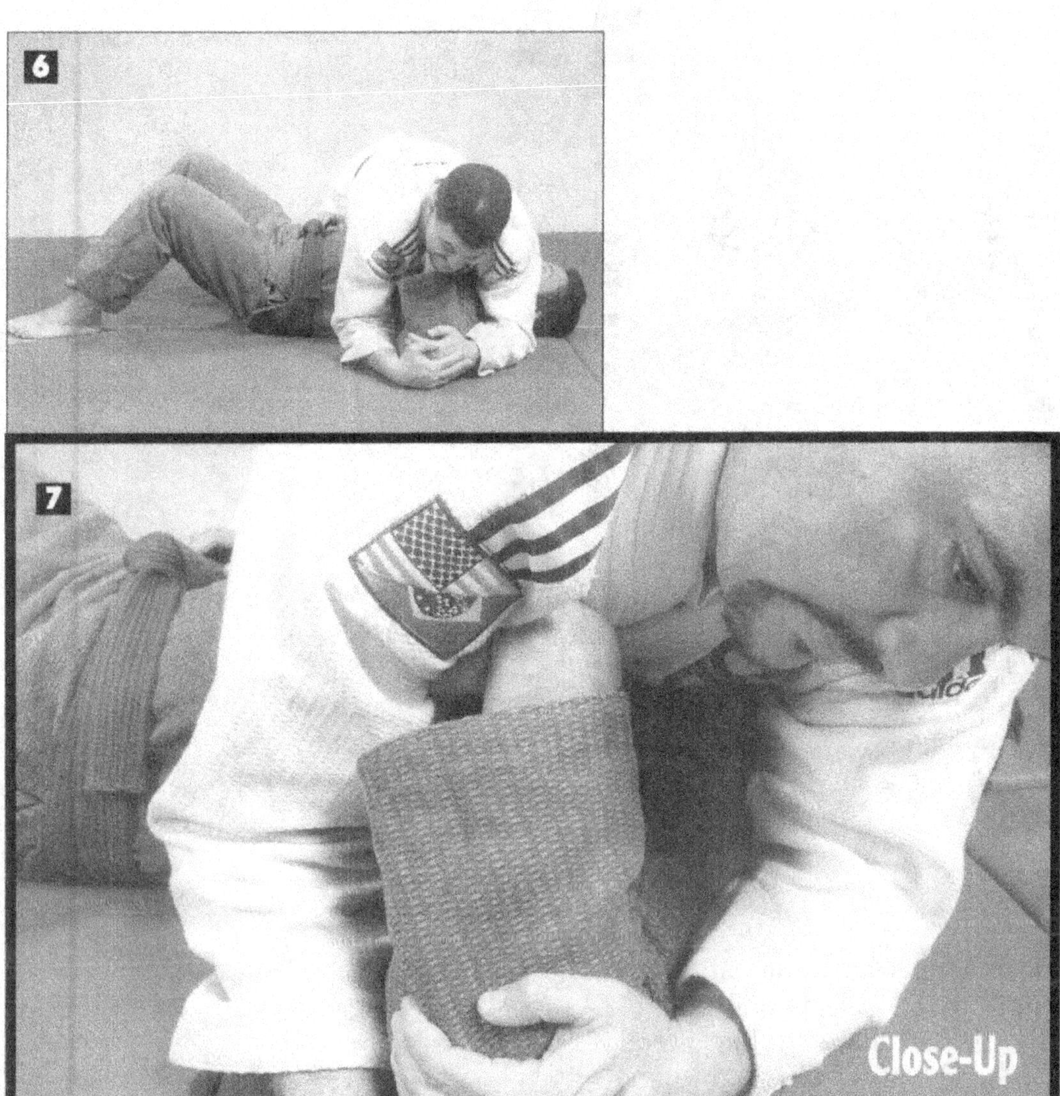

Note that Rigan's right hand is now on his wrist. Rigan pushes to the side (5), breaks the grip (6), and immediately applies a wristlock (*mao-de-vaca*) using his chest (7).

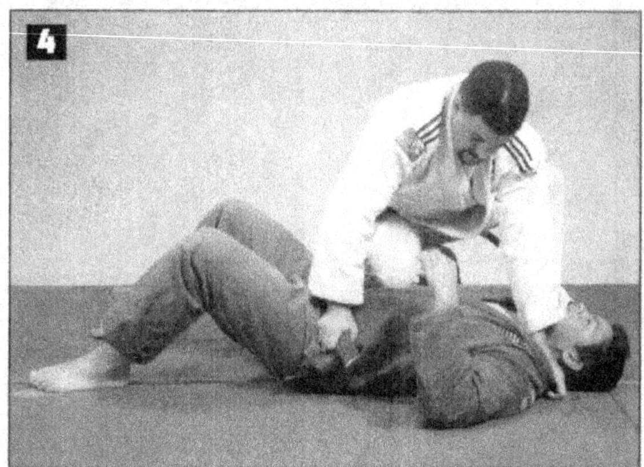

Rigan controls the altercation from the side (1). He grabs his opponent's collar with his left hand and belt with his right hand (2). Rigan pushes himself up (3), and places his right knee on the opponent's stomach (4). The opponent tries to push Rigan's knee away with his left hand (5).

Side Control **15**

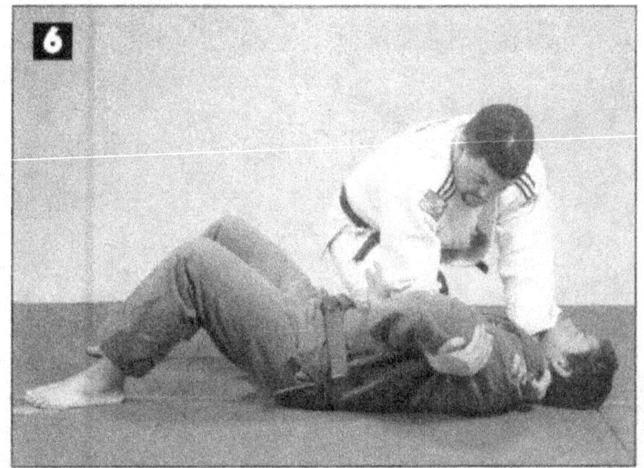

Rigan reacts by hooking the opponent's left arm with his right hand (6), pulling up (7), and executing a straight armlock while standing (8).

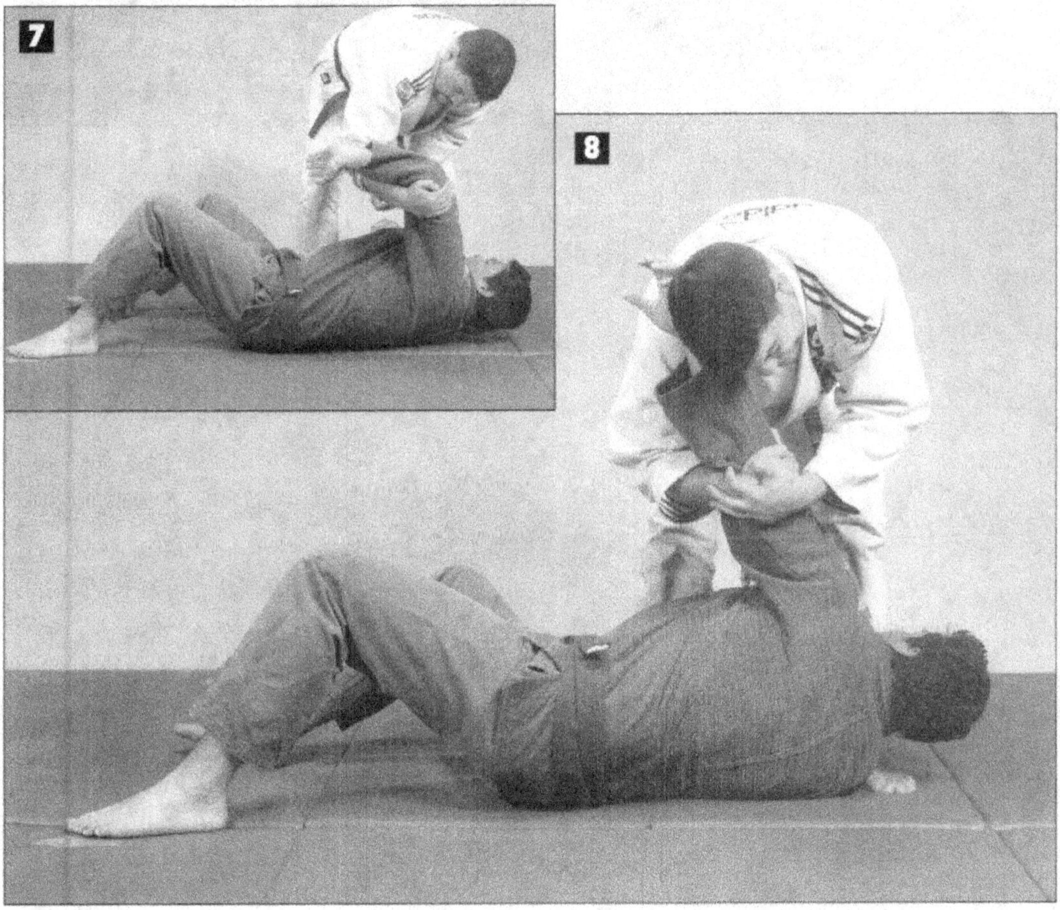

Rigan controls the opponent from the side (1). Note that his left arm is under the opponent's neck. Taking advantage of this positioning, Rigan grabs his right sleeve with his left hand (2). He moves his right forearm to the front of the opponent's neck (3).

Side Control 16

Then he applies pressure (4),
and chokes him out (5).

Rigan controls the opponent from the side (1). Note that his left arm is around the back of the opponent's neck. He switches arms behind the opponent's neck (2), and grabs his left sleeve with his right hand (3). In this close-up, notice how he latches onto the sleeve (4). To execute the choke, Rigan places his left forearm across the front of the opponent's neck (5).

Side Control **17**

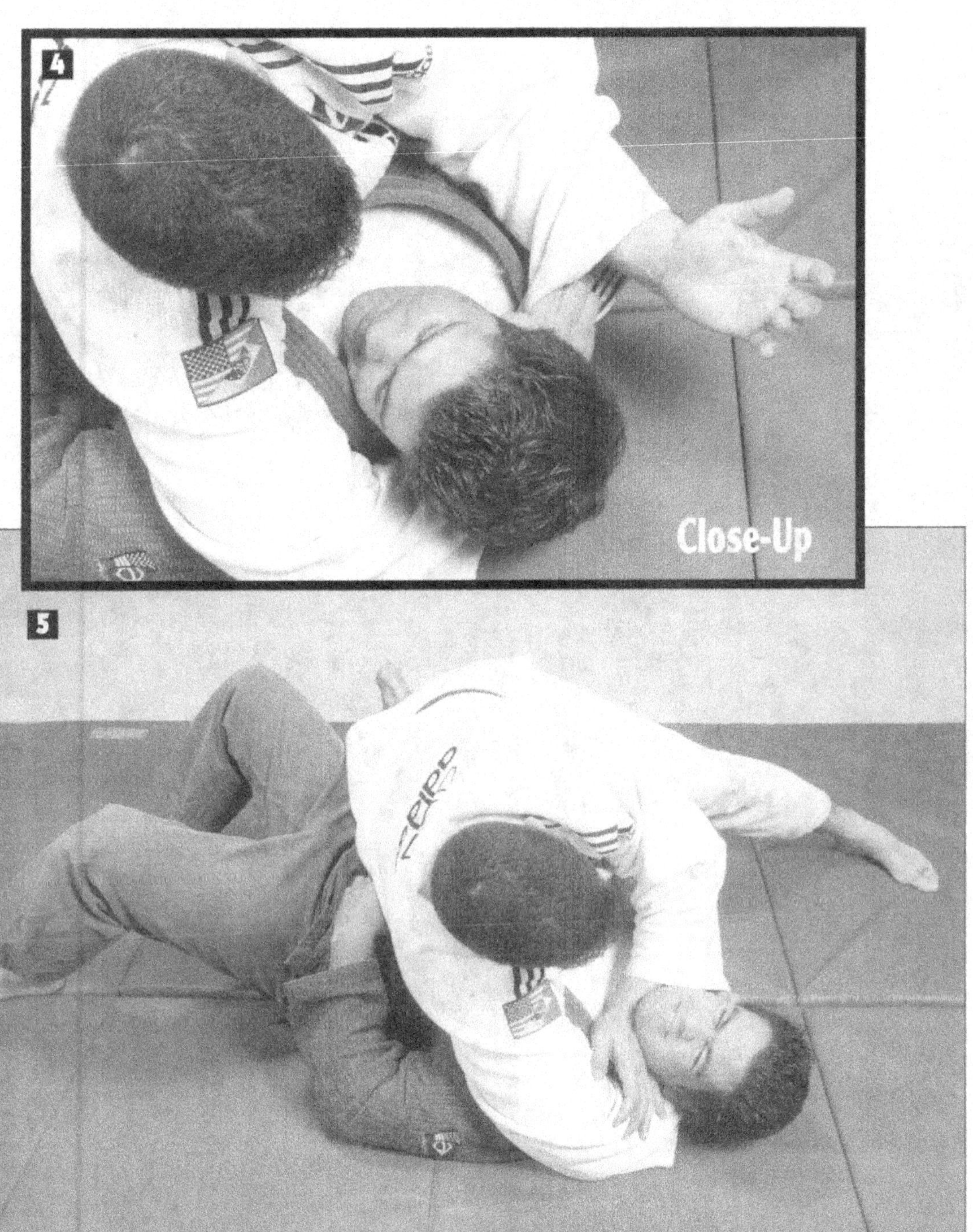

 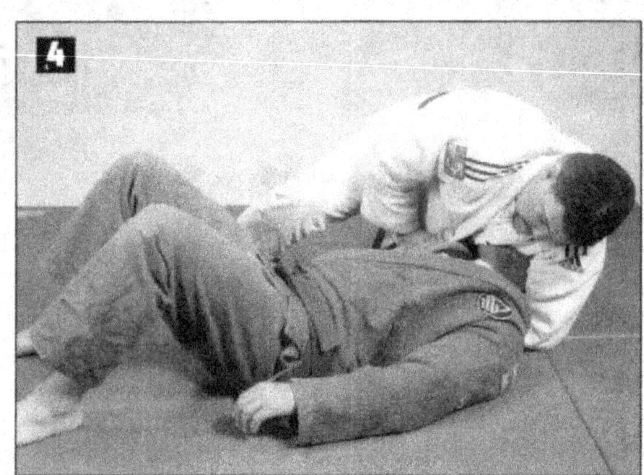

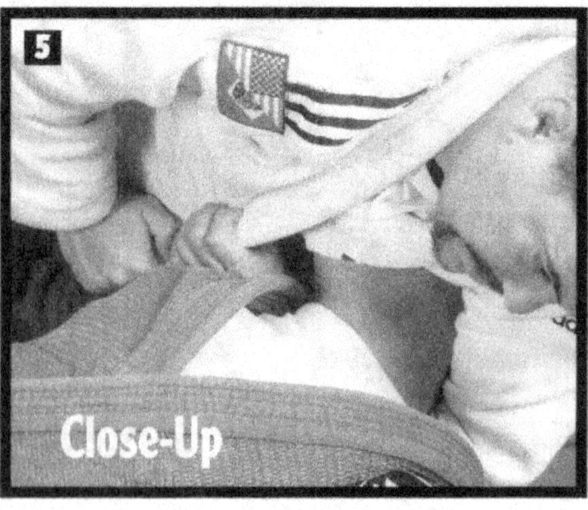

Rigan controls the opponent from the side (1). He wraps his left arm around the opponent's neck (2), loosens his jacket with the right hand (3), and passes it to his left hand (4). A close-up look (5).

Side Control 18

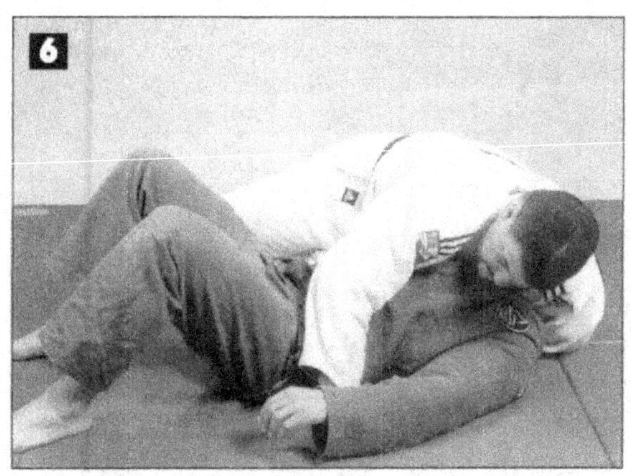

To establish position, he moves his right hand to the other side of the opponent (6), and brings his right leg over (7). Now he can crank on the choke (8).

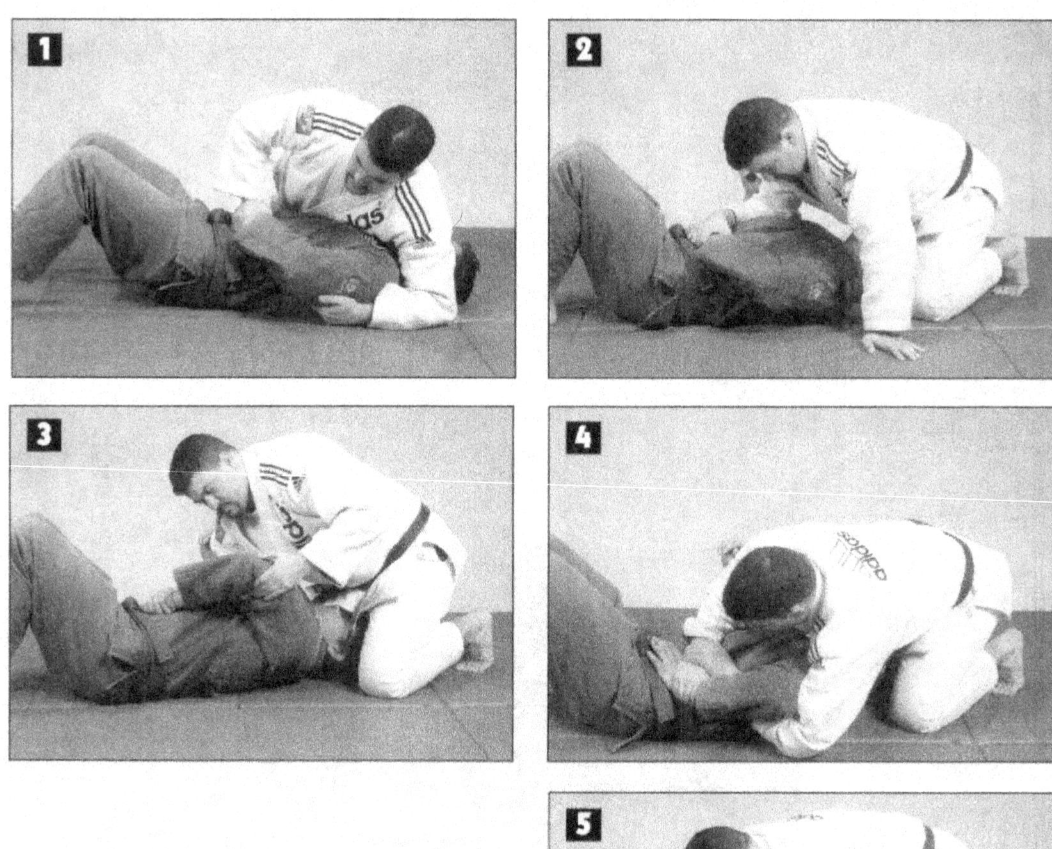

The opponent has a firm grip on his own belt, which Rigan tries to break (1). Rigan circles around and moves toward the opponent's head (2). Using his left hand, Rigan lifts the opponent's left arm (3). Next, Rigan slides his left arm under the opponent's left arm and grabs his own wrist (4). He steps forward with his left leg (5), and pulls

Side Control 19

up hard on the opponent's arm, breaking the grip (6). Rigan then applies a painful bent armlock (7).

Rigan controls the altercation from the side (1). He starts to wrap his left arm around the opponent's neck (2) while he positions his right arm under the opponent's armpit (3). He then grasps his hands together (4). While maintaining the hold, Rigan moves onto his left side (5), and

Side Control **20**

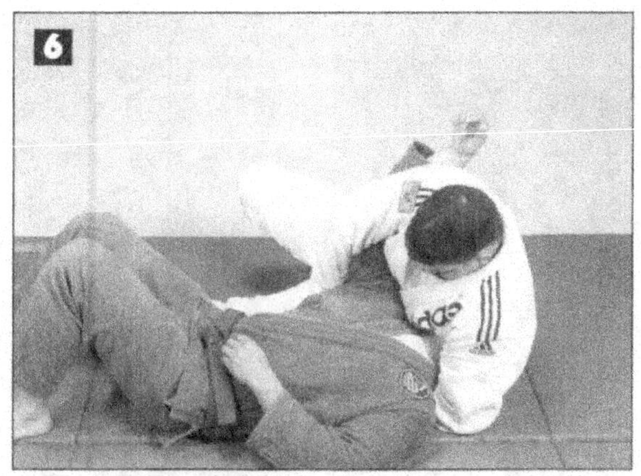

starts bringing his right leg towards the opponent (6). He positions his leg between the opponents legs (7). Notice how he hooks it under the left leg. This position provides leverage for a painful neck crank (8).

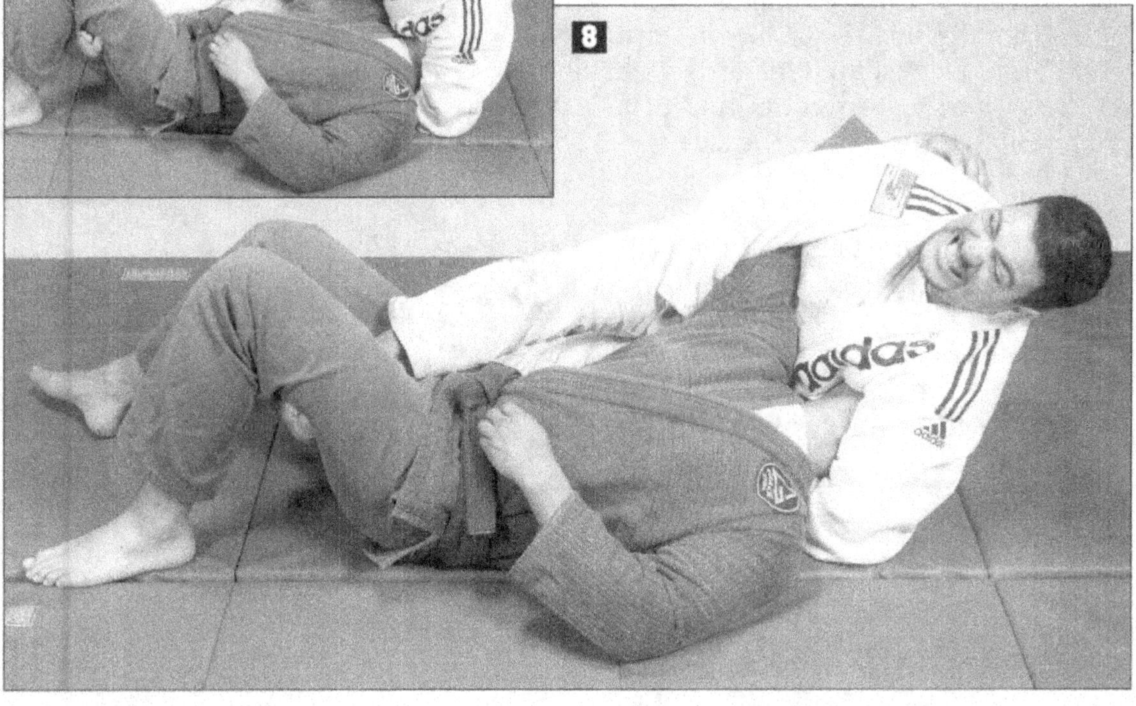

Rigan controls his opponent
from the side (1). While he starts
to stand, he simultaneously grabs
the opponent's right arm (2). He
switches his hips to the side,
brings his body over the opponent's (3), and puts his left leg
over the opponent's left hip (4).
He finishes with a straight armlock (5). It is important to keep
the left leg close to the opponent's armpit so you can create
leverage for the armlock.

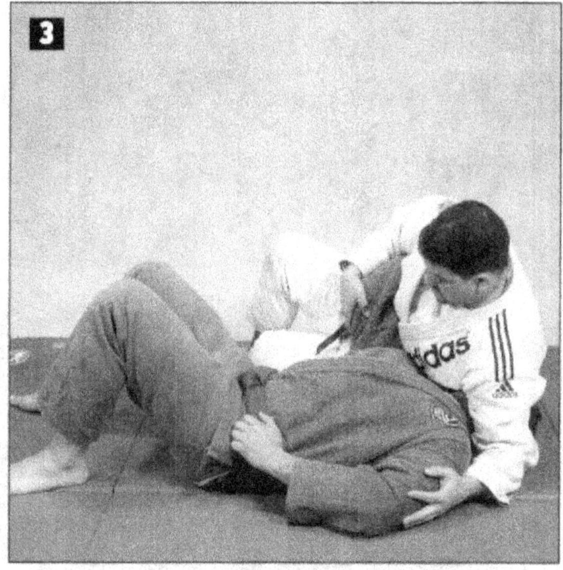

Side Control **21**

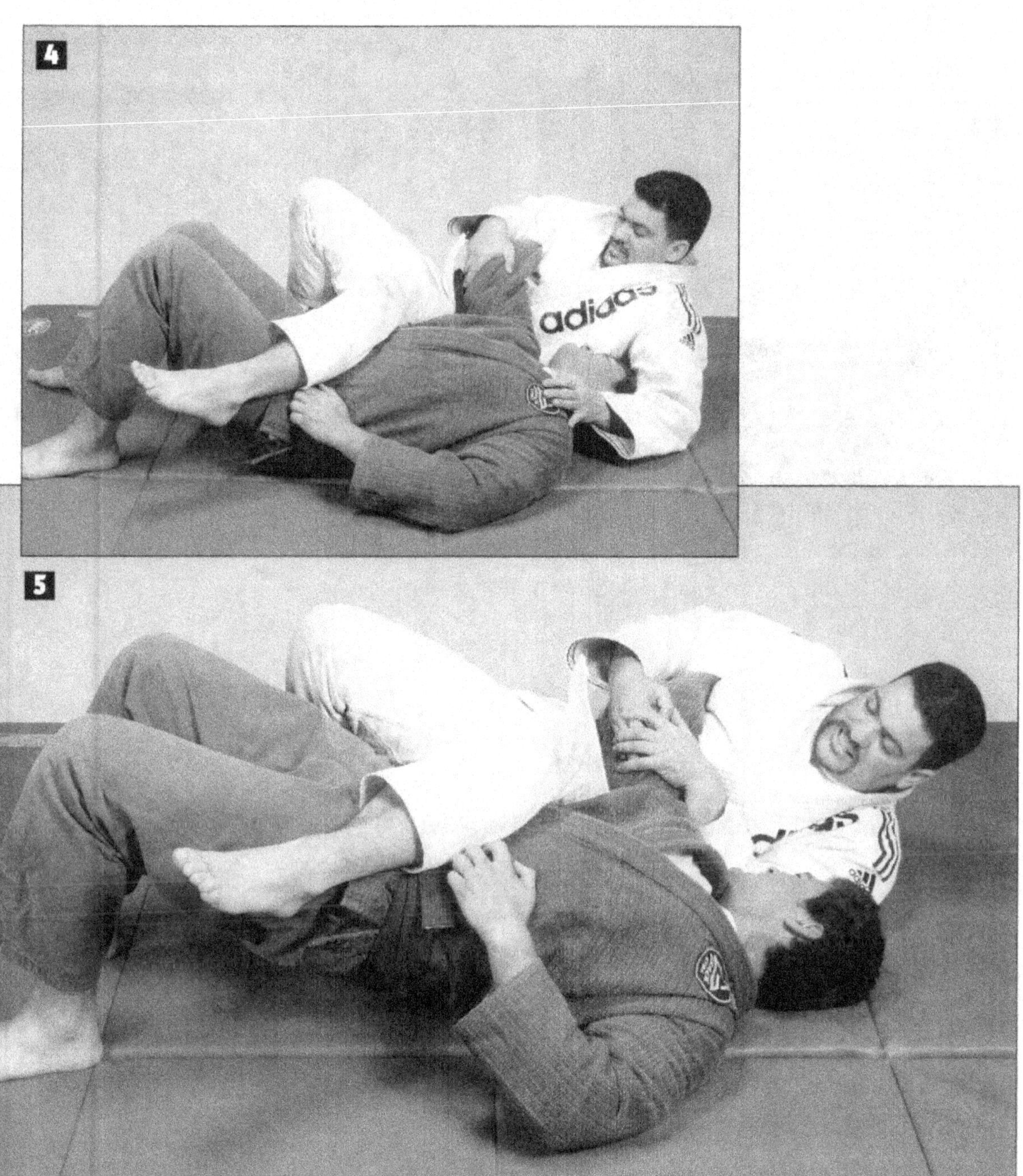

Using his right hand, Rigan breaks the opponent's grip on the belt (1-2). As soon as he breaks the grip, Rigan moves his left leg over the opponent's head (3),

Side Control **22**

and uses his left hand to lift the opponent's left elbow (4). He then applies a painful *kimura* (5).

Rigan maintains side control and breaks the opponent's grip on the belt (1). He slides his left hand under the opponent's arm (2), and then straightens the arm (3). Notice that Rigan has grabbed his right wrist.

Side Control 23

He establishes good leverage (4), and applies a straight armlock (5).

Rigan controls the opponent
from the cross-side position (1).
He loosens his gi (2), and moves
it to the other side (3) so he can
reach it with his right hand,
which is under the opponent's
left arm (4). He passes the
uniform to his left hand (5-6),

Side Control **24**

which is under the opponent's neck. Rigan immediately brings his left knee up against the opponent's neck (7), and applies a finishing choke (8).

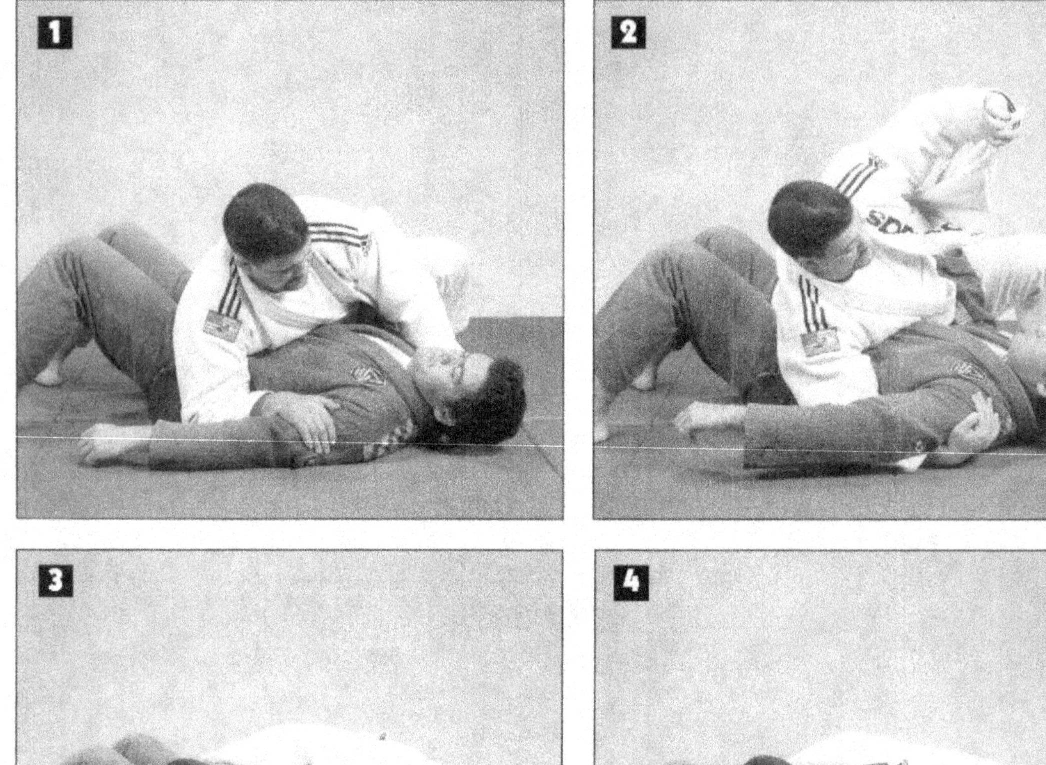

Rigan controls the opponent from the side (1). He loosens his gi (2), and moves it across his opponent (3) so he can reach it with his right hand (4).

Side Control 25

He passes it again to his left hand (5), and switches his hips to trap his opponent (6).

continued

continued from page 203

Rigan rolls over (7) his left
shoulder (8) all the way to the
front (9-10).

Side Control **25**

He concludes with a finishing choke (11).

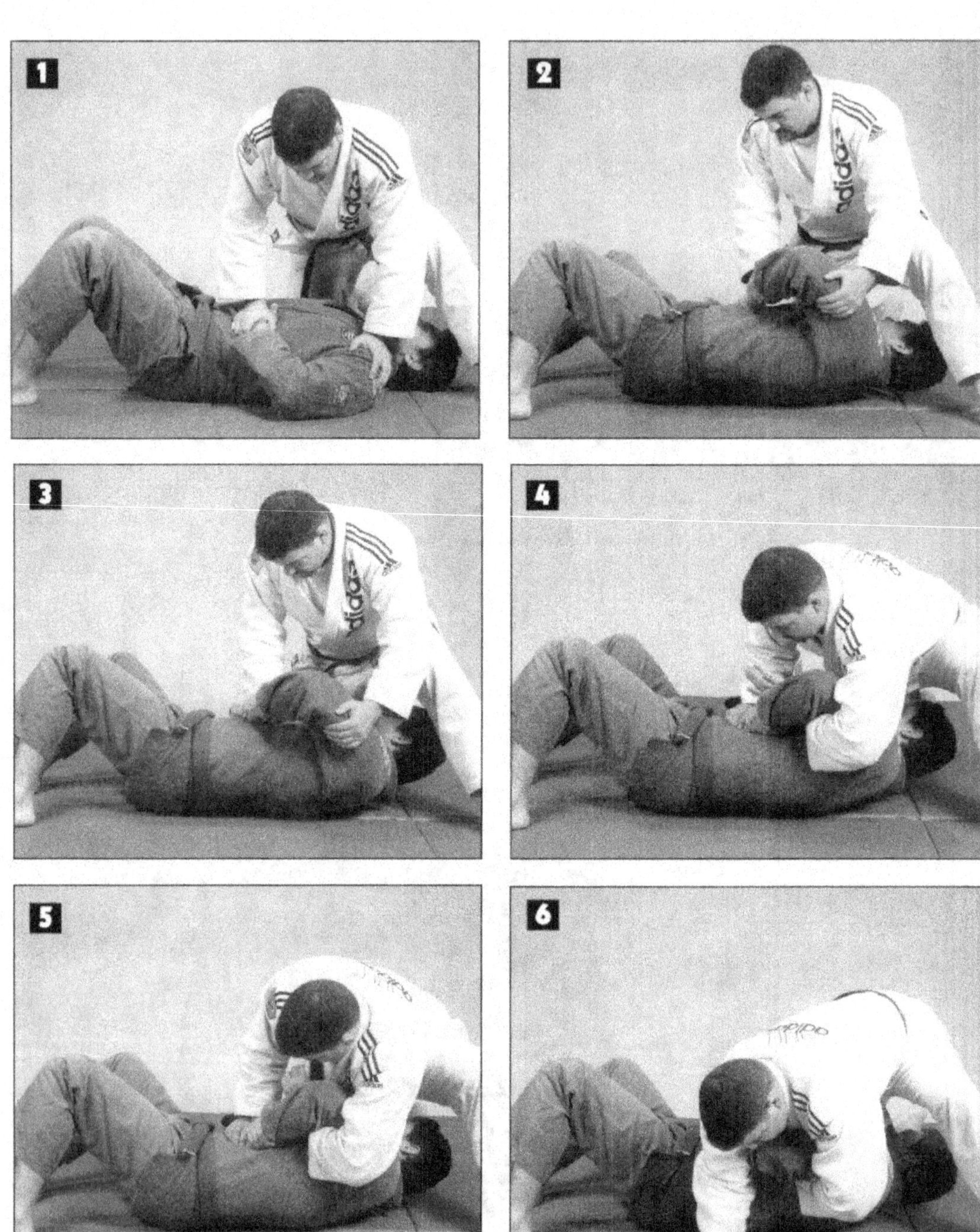

Side Control 26

To break the opponent's grip, Rigan starts to stand (1). The opponent resists (2), and tries to bring his arm back down (3). Rigan puts his left arm under the opponent's left arm (4), and applies pressure to break the grip (5). This doesn't work because the opponent's hands are still too close to his body (6). Rigan establishes his position (7), and moves his right leg forward (8). He uses his right elbow to create leverage so he can apply a bent armlock (9).

Rigan maintains control from the side, but the opponent turns to the side to avoid the attack (1). Rigan loosens the opponent's gi with his right hand (2), and grabs the uniform with his left hand (3).

Side Control **27**

Notice that he traps the opponent's left arm while doing this. Using his right hand to control the opponent's right arm (4), Rigan prepares for the finishing move (5).

continued

continued from page 209

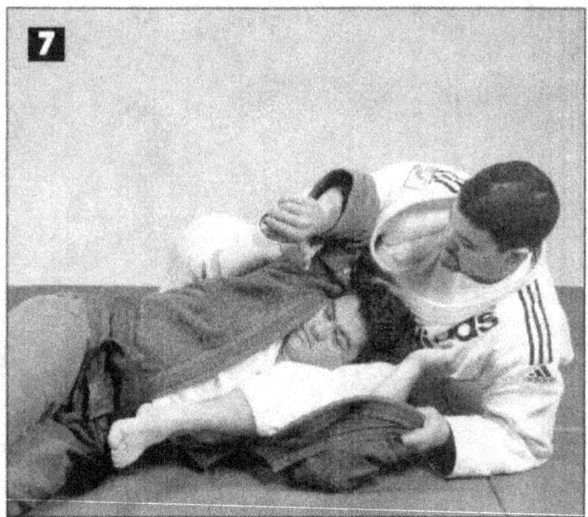

First, he moves his left leg next to the opponent's neck (6). Meanwhile, he controls the left arm with his left hand (7). He crosses his left leg over the opponent's chest (8), hooks

Side Control **27**

his left instep under the back of the right leg (9), and applies a *triangle* choke from the back (10).

Controlling the oppo-
nent from the side,
Rigan loosens the oppo-
nent's gi with his right
hand (1), and passes it to
his left hand (2), trap-
ping the opponent's left
arm with the gi (3).

Side Control **28**

He slides his right hand in to grab the collar (4), applies pressure and executes the choke (5).

Rigan controls his opponent from the side (1). He sits up, slides his hips to the right and traps the opponent's right hand (2).

Side Control **29**

He brings his left leg over the opponent's head, applies pressure and executes a straight armlock (3). It's important to keep your legs firmly over the opponent's arm. Also, don't put your left leg too far from the opponent's head; otherwise, he'll be able to escape.

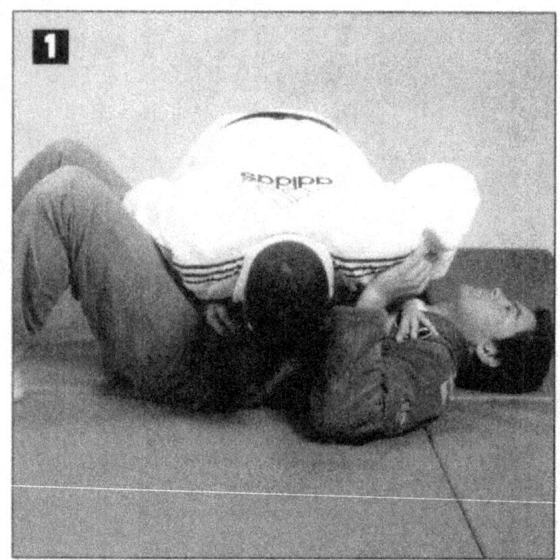 

Rigan controls the opponent from the side (1). He moves slightly to the left (2) so he can switch his hips (3). Meanwhile, he tightens the grip on the opponent's collar (4).

Side Control **30**

He brings his left leg over the opponent's head, pulls hard on the uniform and chokes him out (5). In this close-up, notice that Rigan creates the choke by using the gi and his left foot (6).

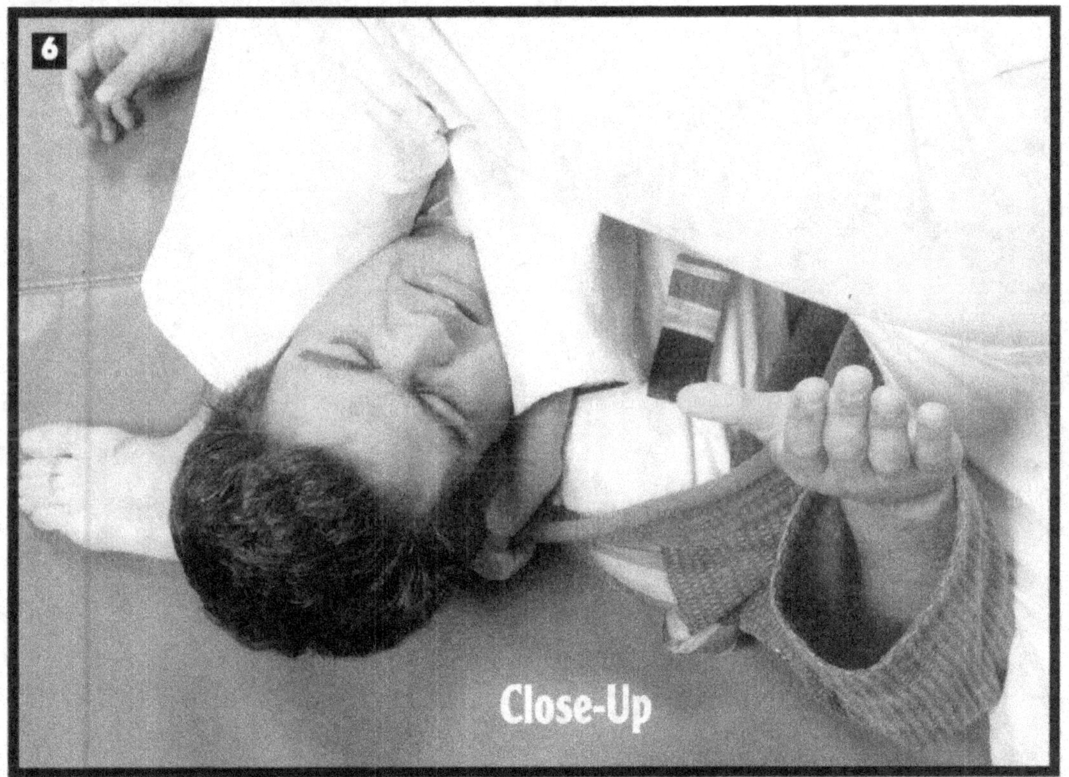

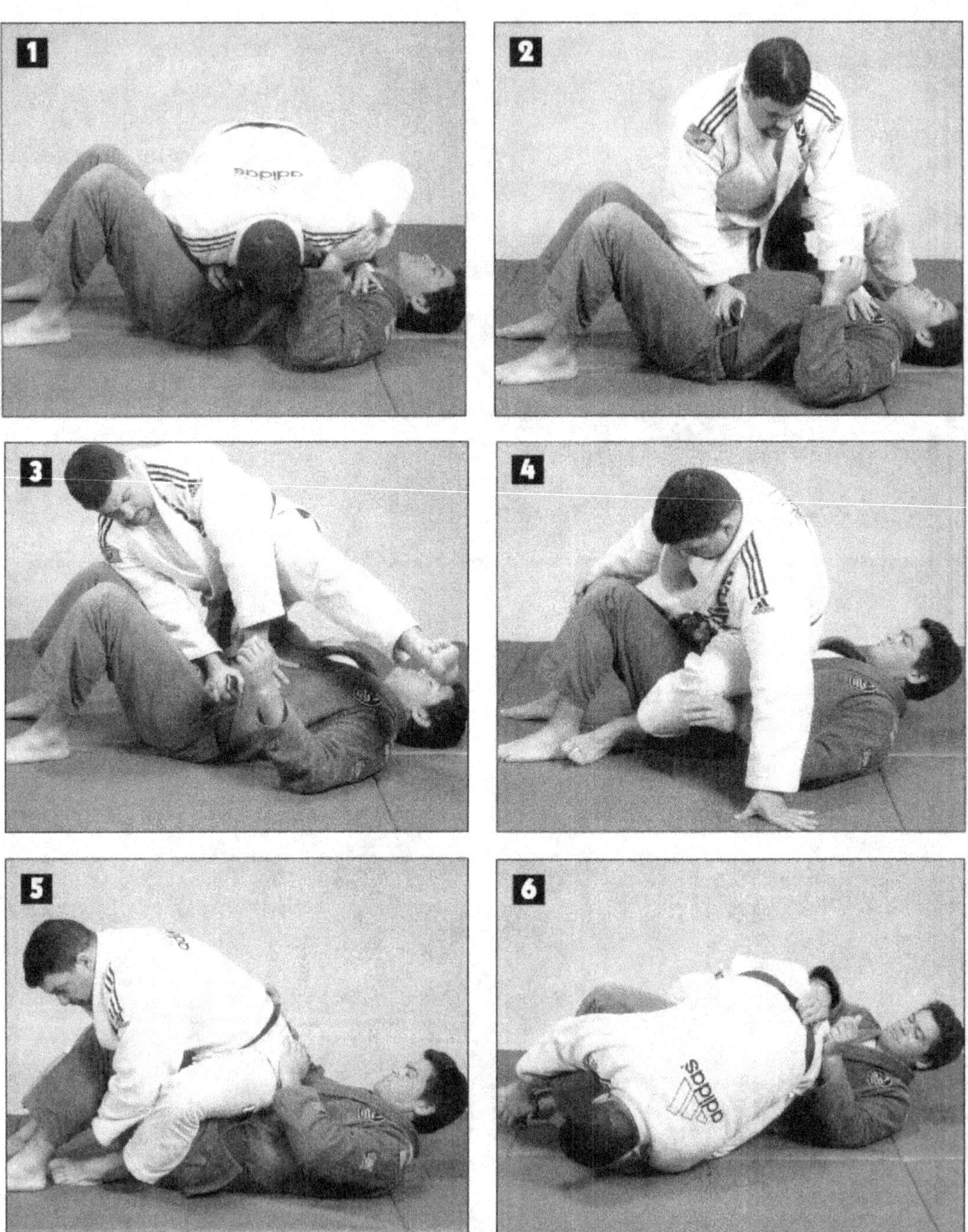

Side Control 31

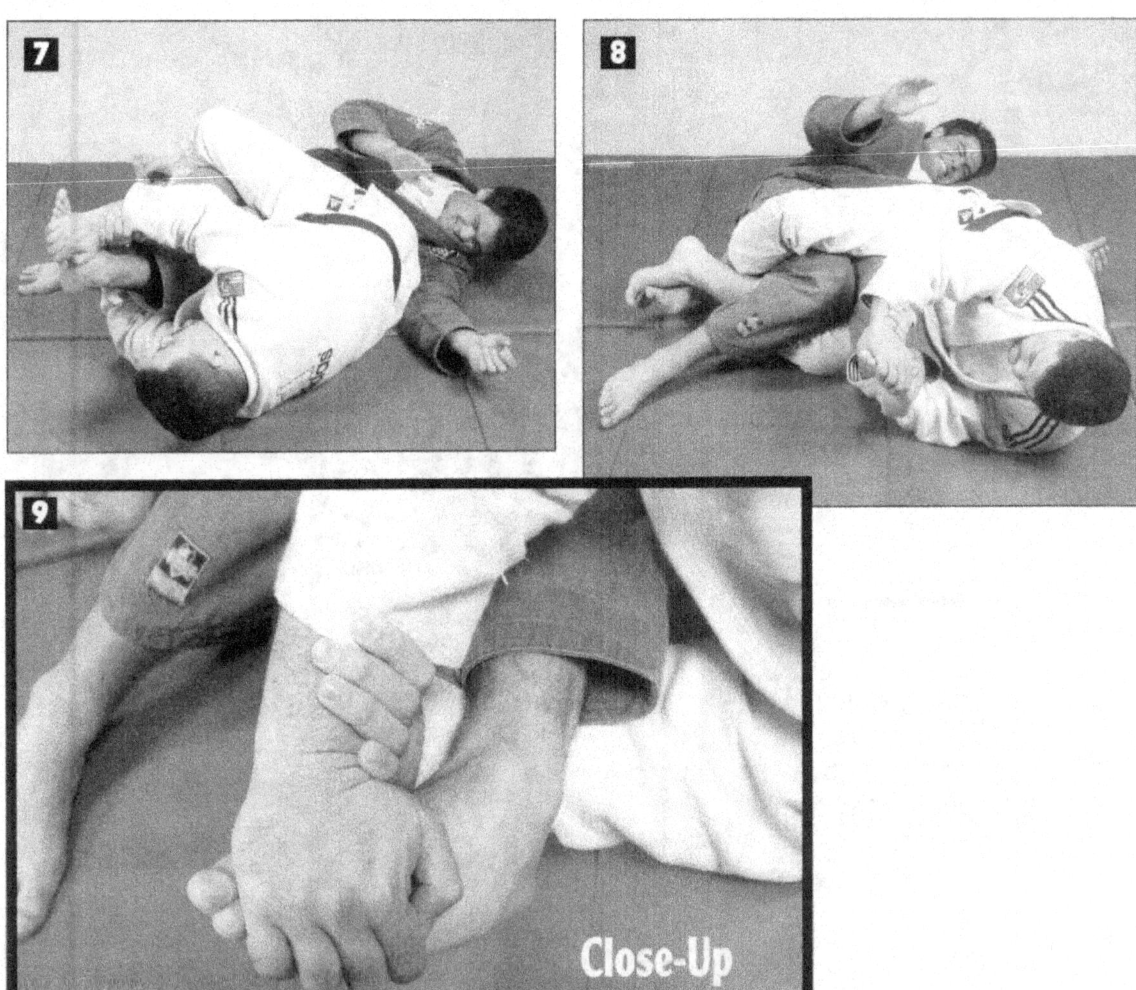

Rigan controls the opponent from the side (1). He starts to stand (2), he swings his left leg over the opponent's body (3), and sits on the opponent's stomach (4). Rigan grabs the opponent's left foot with his left hand (5), and rolls to the left (6). He uses his right hand (7) to create a "Figure 4" anklelock (8). A close-up (9).

While controlling from the side (1), Rigan brings his right knee over the opponent's stomach as he secures the left arm (2).

Side Control **32**

He leans forward, allowing his body weight to drop (3). He straightens the opponent's left arm and applies a painful armlock (4).

Rigan tries to control his opponent from the side, but this one rolls away from him (1). Rather than chase him, Rigan springs up, mounts the opponent (2) and sits on him (3-4). He establishes the half-mount, grabs the opponent's uniform with his right hand (5)

and passes it to his left hand (6). By moving his right hand over the right side of the opponent's neck and pulling the gi with his left hand, Rigan chokes him (7).

Rigan controls the opponent
from the side (1). Rigan uses his
left arm to trap the opponent's
left arm (2), and then raises up
and places his left knee on the
opponent's chest (3).

Side Control 34

Using his right hand to establish position, Rigan passes his right leg over the opponent's head (4), leans back and executes an armlock (5).

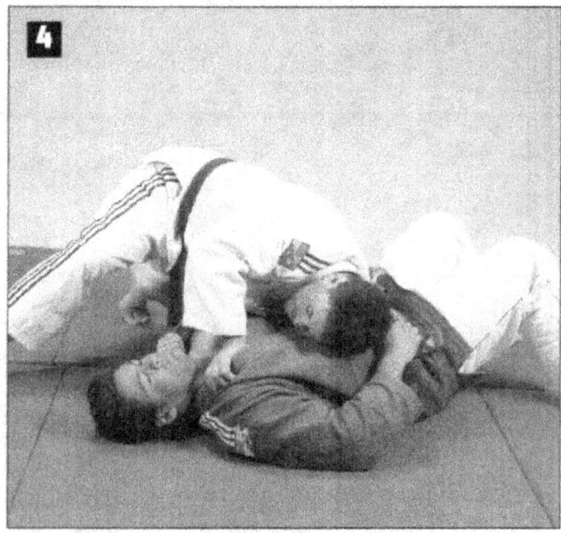

From a side control (1), Rigan moves his hips back and creates room to move his left arm under the opponent's left arm so he can grab the opponent's collar (2). He slides his right hand — with the palm down — onto the other side of the collar (3). He maintains a tight grip as he prepares to finish off his adversary (4).

Side Control **35**

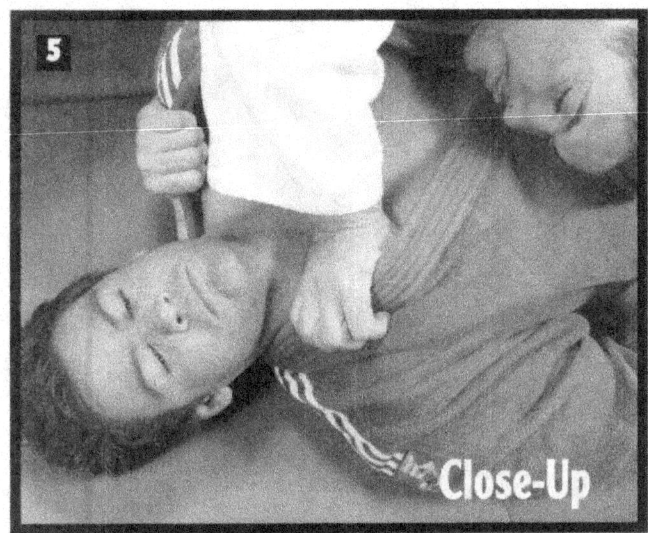

A close look at the action (5). Rigan lowers his forearm and chokes the opponent (6).

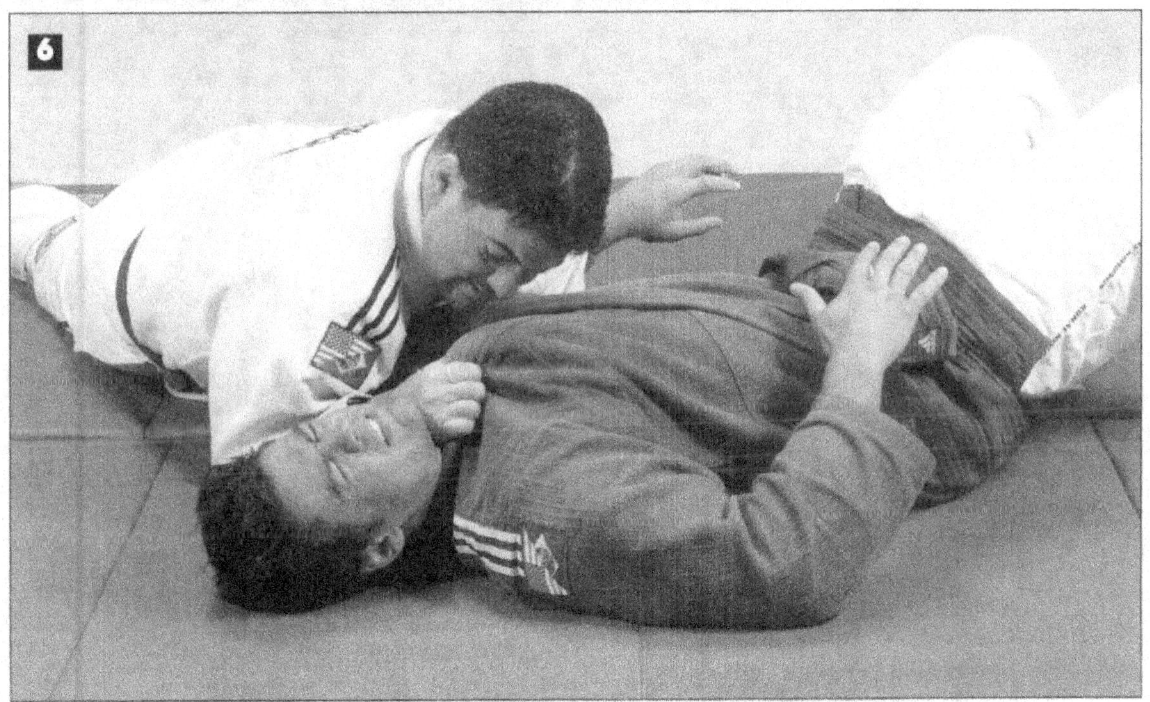

Rigan tries to establish control from the side, but his opponent turns and grabs his left leg (1). Rigan circles to the right (2), and grabs the opponent's right arm (3). Rigan leans backwards (4).

Side Control 36

Then he pulls the arm all the way down (5), and finishes with a straight armlock (6).

Rigan controls the altercation from the side (1) and then uses his left hand to push the opponent's left wrist down (2). The opponent uses his right hand to stop Rigan (3), who reacts by grabbing the opponent's hand (4) and pushing it down so he can trap it with his left leg (5).

Side Control 37

Rigan goes back to the left wrist (6), and applies a finishing bent armlock (7).

Rigan controls his opponent from the side (1). He slides his right knee onto the opponent's chest and grabs the right sleeve (2).

Side Control 38

Rigan starts to lean backwards, applies pressure (3), moves his left leg over the opponent's neck and finishes with an armlock (4).

Rigan controls the opponent from the side (1). Using a reverse grip with his left hand, Rigan grabs the right side of the opponent's collar (2), and begins to circle his left leg towards the opponent's head (3). Once he establishes his position (4), Rigan begins to apply pressure by dropping his body

Side Control **39**

weight (5). Controlling the opponent's left arm with his right hand, Rigan applies even greater pressure and chokes him out (6).

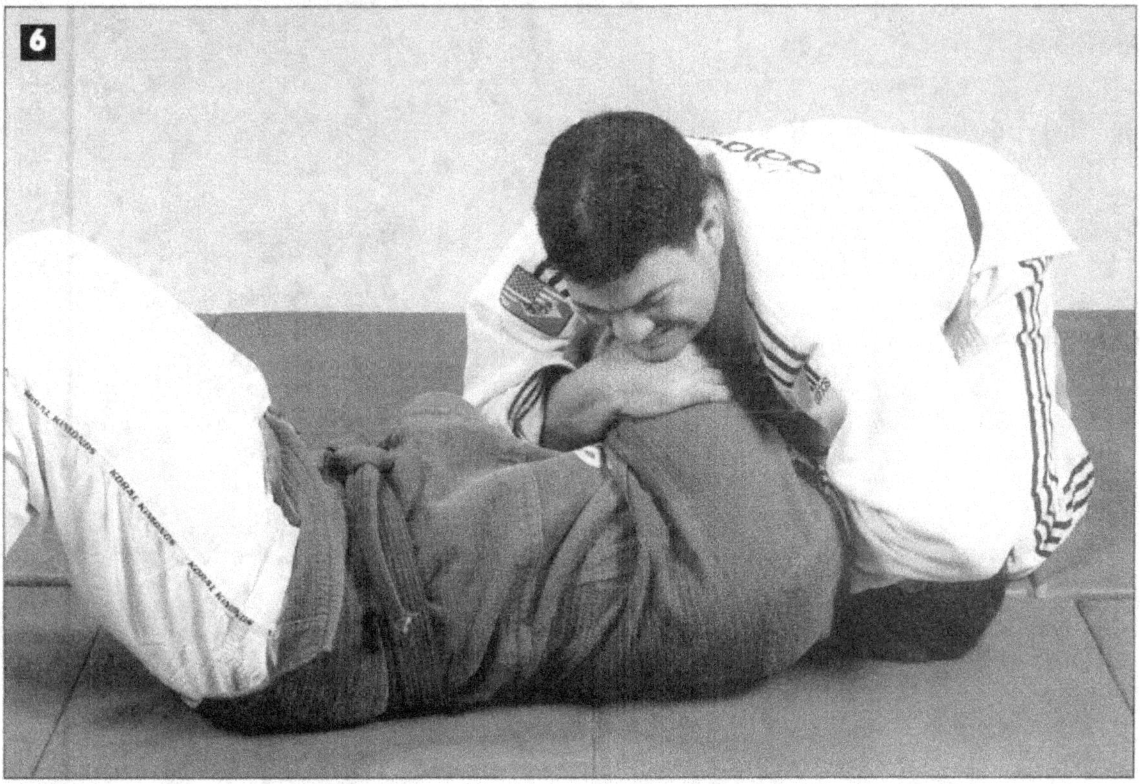

While controlling the clash from the side, Rigan passes his left hand behind the opponent's neck (1), and his right hand over the chest (2). He applies pressure to execute a finishing choke (3).

Side Control **40**

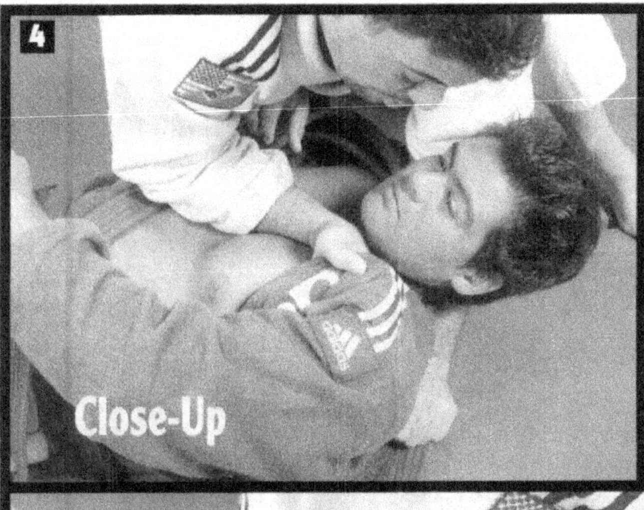

The close-ups show the details (4-5).

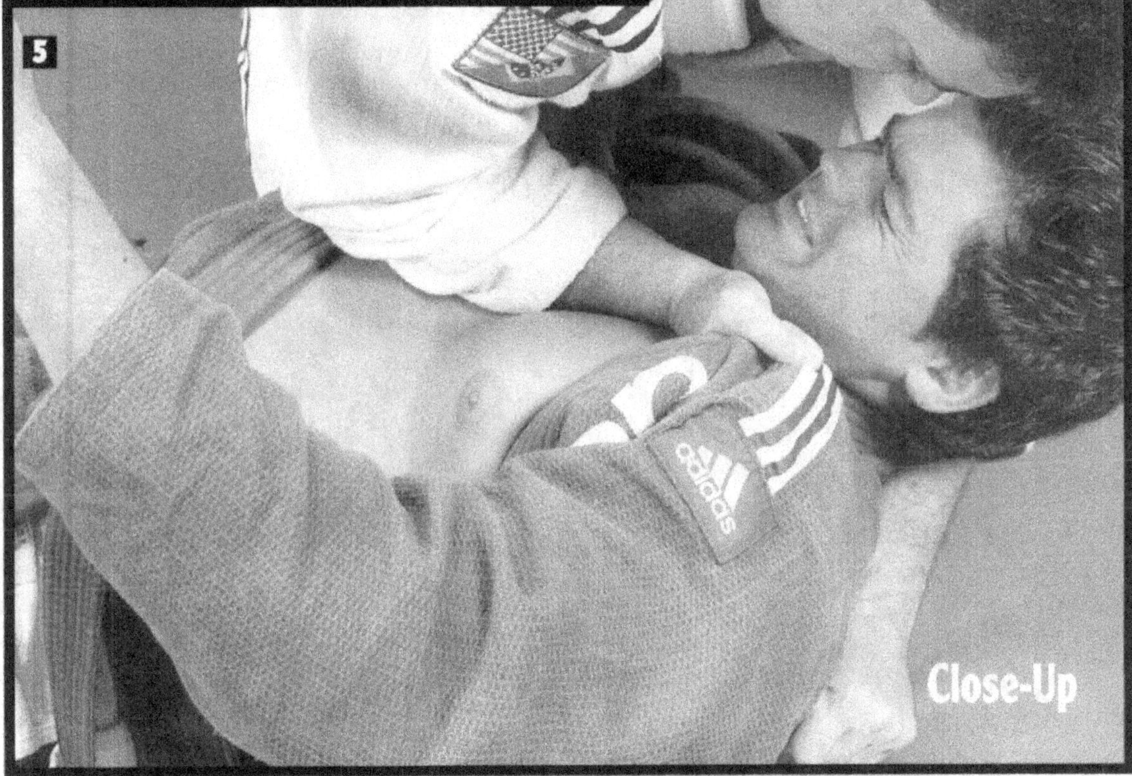

Rigan controls the opponent from the side (1). Notice that his left hand is under the opponent's head. Rigan traps the right arm as he simultaneously moves his left leg to the front (2). Rigan hooks the opponent's left arm with his left foot (3), starts

Side Control 41

to lean backwards (4),
and executes an
armlock (5).

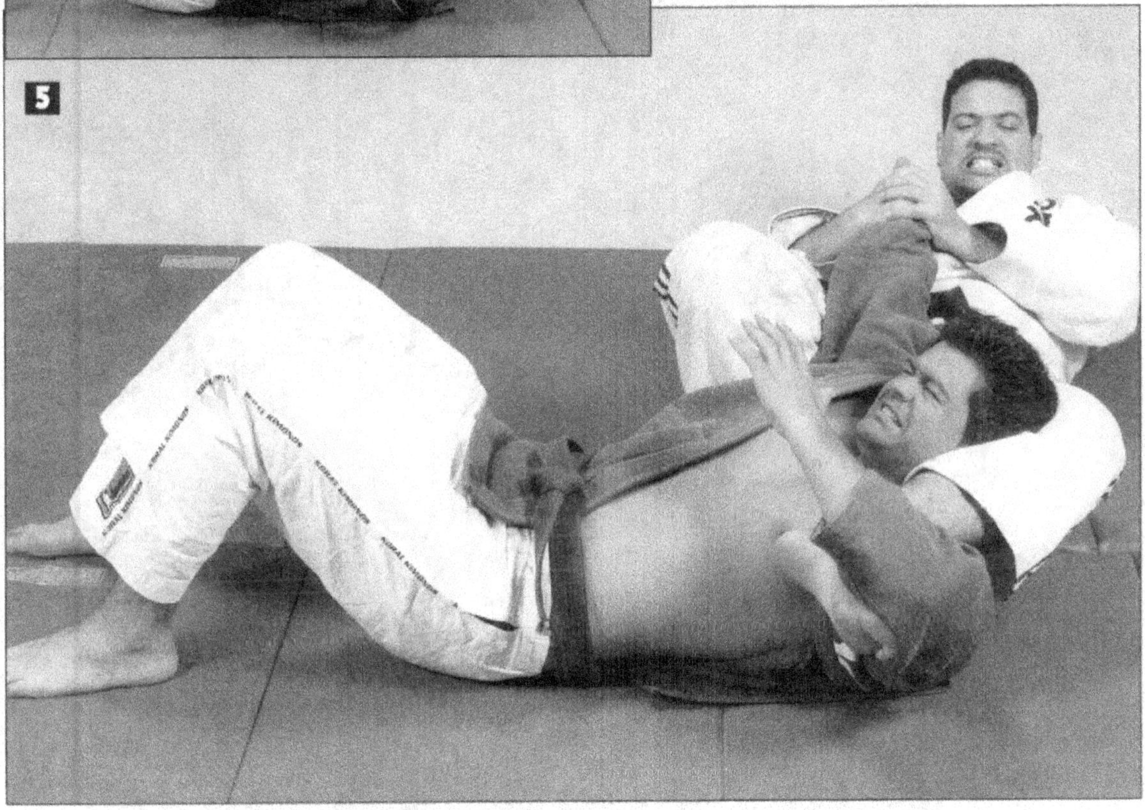

Maintaining a tight grip on his opponent's jacket, Rigan establishes control from the side (1). Using his right arm, Rigan traps the opponent's left arm (2). As soon as Rigan tries to initiate the offensive to mount him, the opponent raises his right knee and stops Rigan cold (3). In response, Rigan grabs his own foot and pulls the opponent's jacket with his left hand (4). This enables him to pass the opponent's knee (5), mount him (6) and establish control (7).

Side Control **42**

Rigan controls the opponent from the side with a tight grip on the jacket (1). Notice Rigan's left hand under the opponent's neck. Using his right arm, Rigan traps the opponent's right arm (2). This enables Rigan to bring him closer (3). Rigan pulls the opponent up (4) so he is between his legs (5).

242

Side Control 43

Rigan now has full control from the back (6). Rigan uses his left hand to grab the right side of the collar (7) and applies a finishing choke (8).

Controlling the altercation from
the side, Rigan reaches for the
opponent's left arm (1), and pulls
it closer (2). Rigan then moves
his right leg over the opponent
(3) as he leans forward to create
space (4-5).

Side Control **44**

He brings his left leg over the opponent's head (6). He can now apply a straight armlock (7).

Rigan controls the opponent from
the side (1). He raises his hips (2)
so he can reach under his right leg
and grab the opponent's right
hand (3). Rigan sits (4), leans forward to roll (5), spins 180

Side Control 45

6

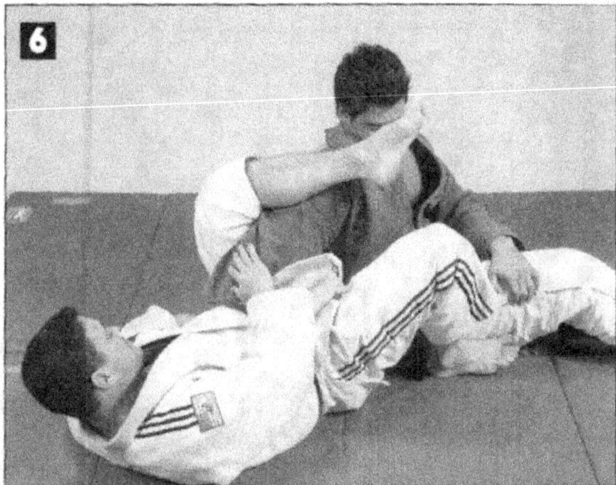

degrees (6) and applies an *omoplata* from the side (7).

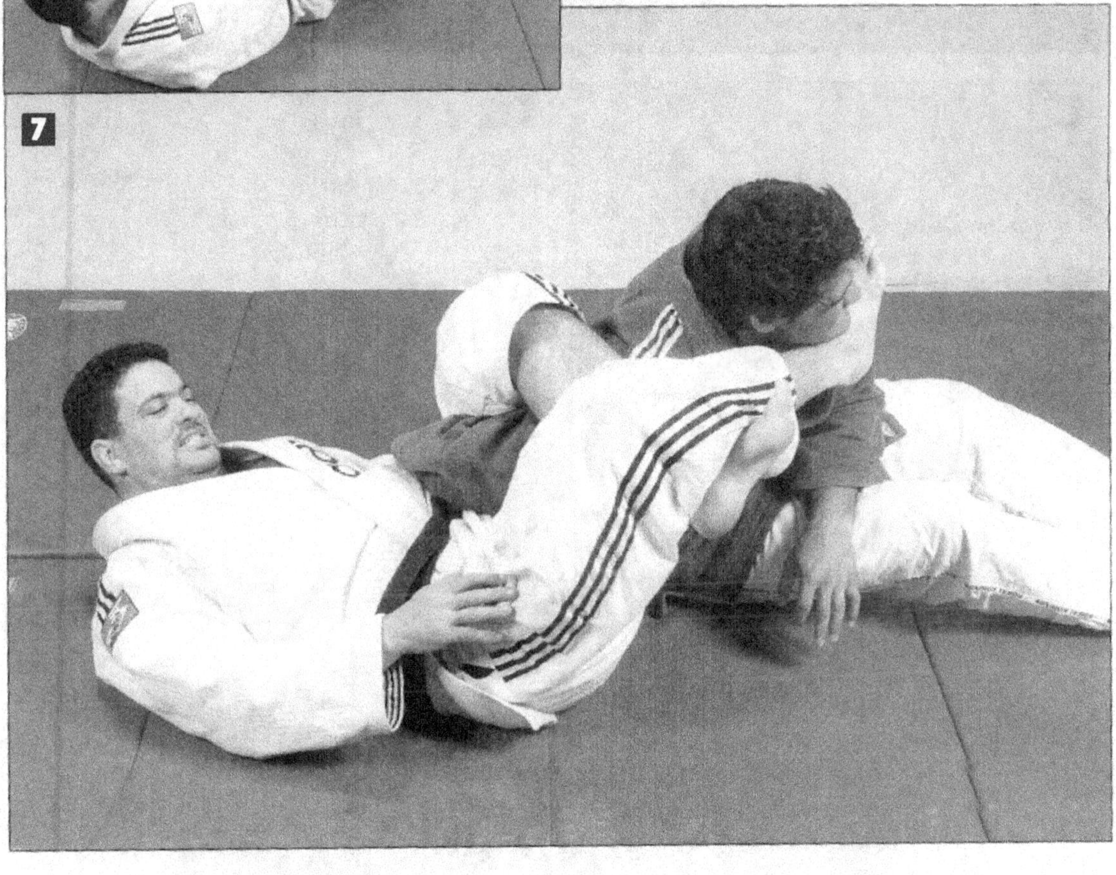
7

Rigan establishes control from the side (1). He raises his hips to create space (2) so he reach under his right leg and grab the opponent's right sleeve (3). Rigan turns away from the opponent (4), and moves his left leg close to the opponent's head (5).

Side Control 46

He leans back (6), and applies an armlock (7).

Rigan grabs the opponent's right arm (1), and then swings his right leg to the back (2), forcing the opponent to turn face down (3).

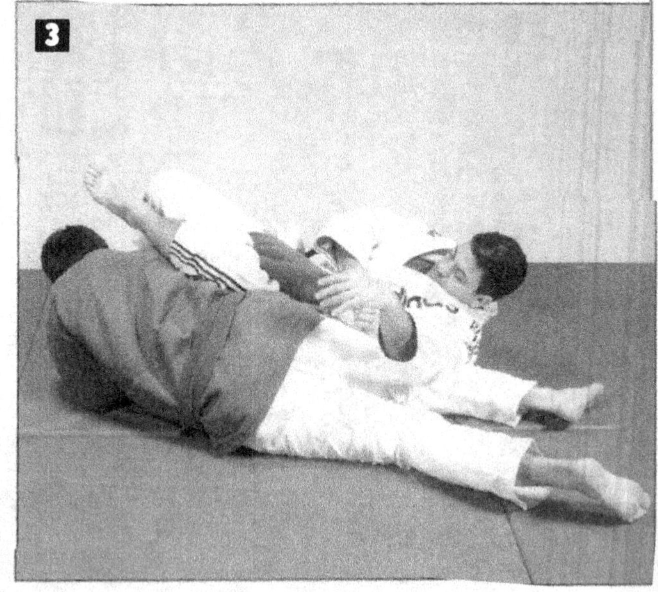

Side Control 47

He uses his left leg to trap the opponent's arm and then grabs the opponent's right foot (4). He finishes with a painful anklelock (5).

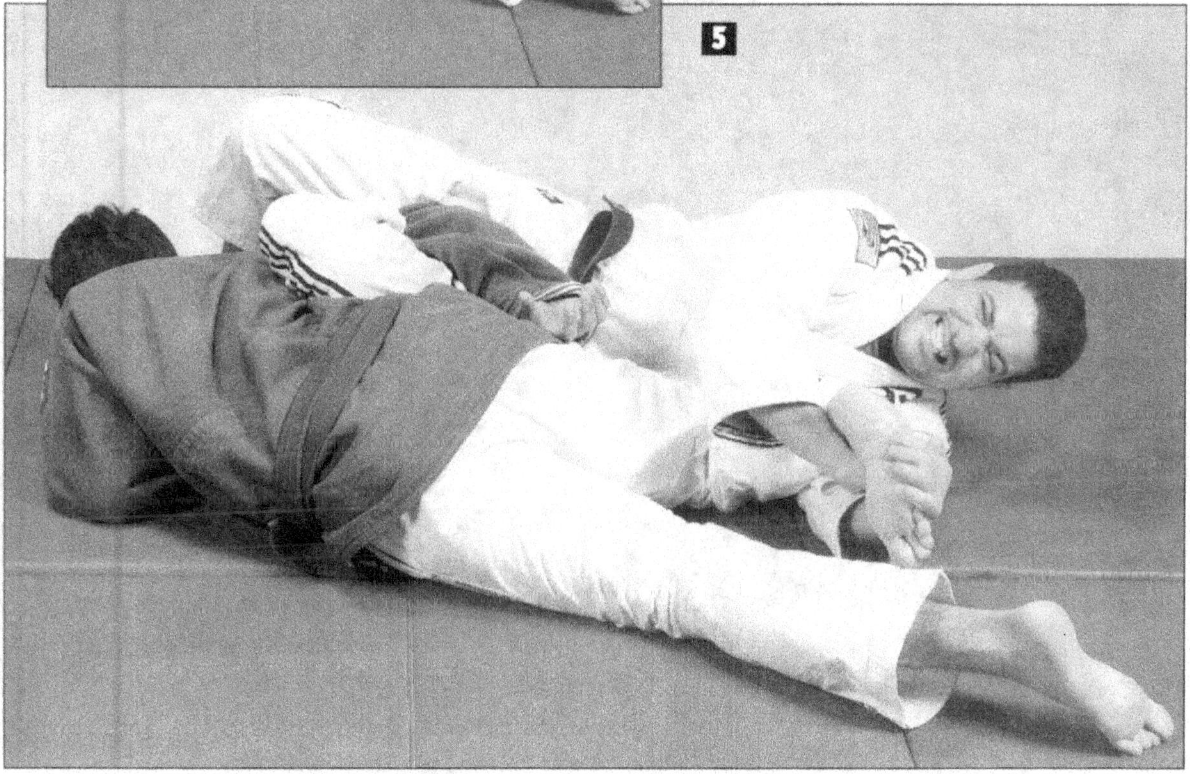

Rigan grabs the opponent's right arm and leans forward (1). He rolls to the side (2), which forces the opponent upright (3). Rigan swivels his hips so he alters his direction slightly (4).

Side Control 48

He then hooks his left foot under his right knee (5), and applies a straight armlock (6).

Rigan grabs the opponent's right arm (1) and rolls onto his left shoulder (2). This movement forces the opponent upright and to the front (3). Rigan then grabs the opponent's left arm (4-5).

Side Control **49**

Then he pulls on the opponent's collar, submitting him from behind (6).

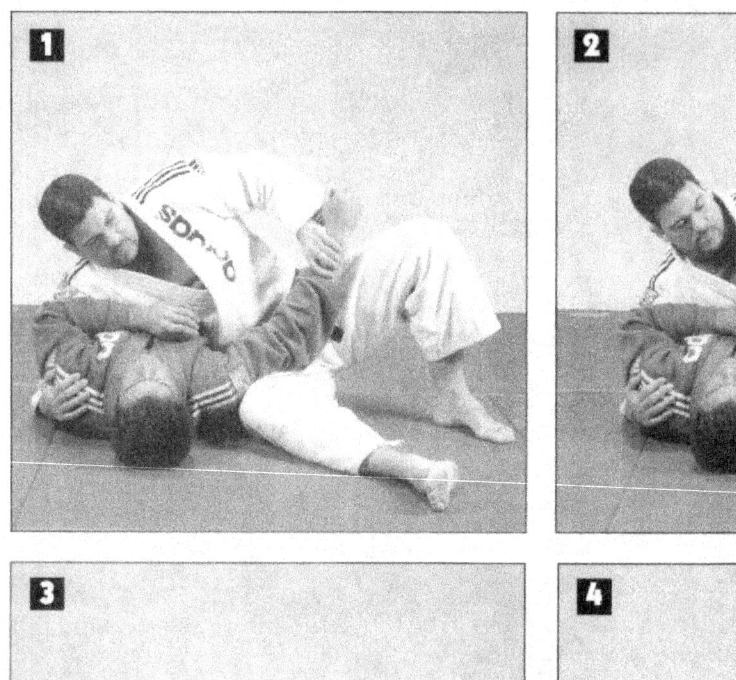

Rigan controls the opponent from the side (1). Notice that he has grabbed the opponent's right arm. Rigan forces the arm under his left leg (2), and pulls the opponent towards him (3). Rigan quickly shifts his body, wraps his left arm around the opponent's neck and leans on him (4).

Side Control 50

Grabbing his left hand with the right, Rigan applies pressure (5), and submits his opponent (6).

Rigan establishes control from the side (1). Note that he's clenching the opponent's right arm with his left hand. Rigan puts the right arm under his left leg (2), pulls the opponent's left arm (3), and maintains control by applying pressure with his body (4).

Side Control **51**

With both of the opponent's arms trapped, Rigan adjusts his hips (5), brings his right knee up (6), mounts the opponent (7), and applies a finishing choke (8).

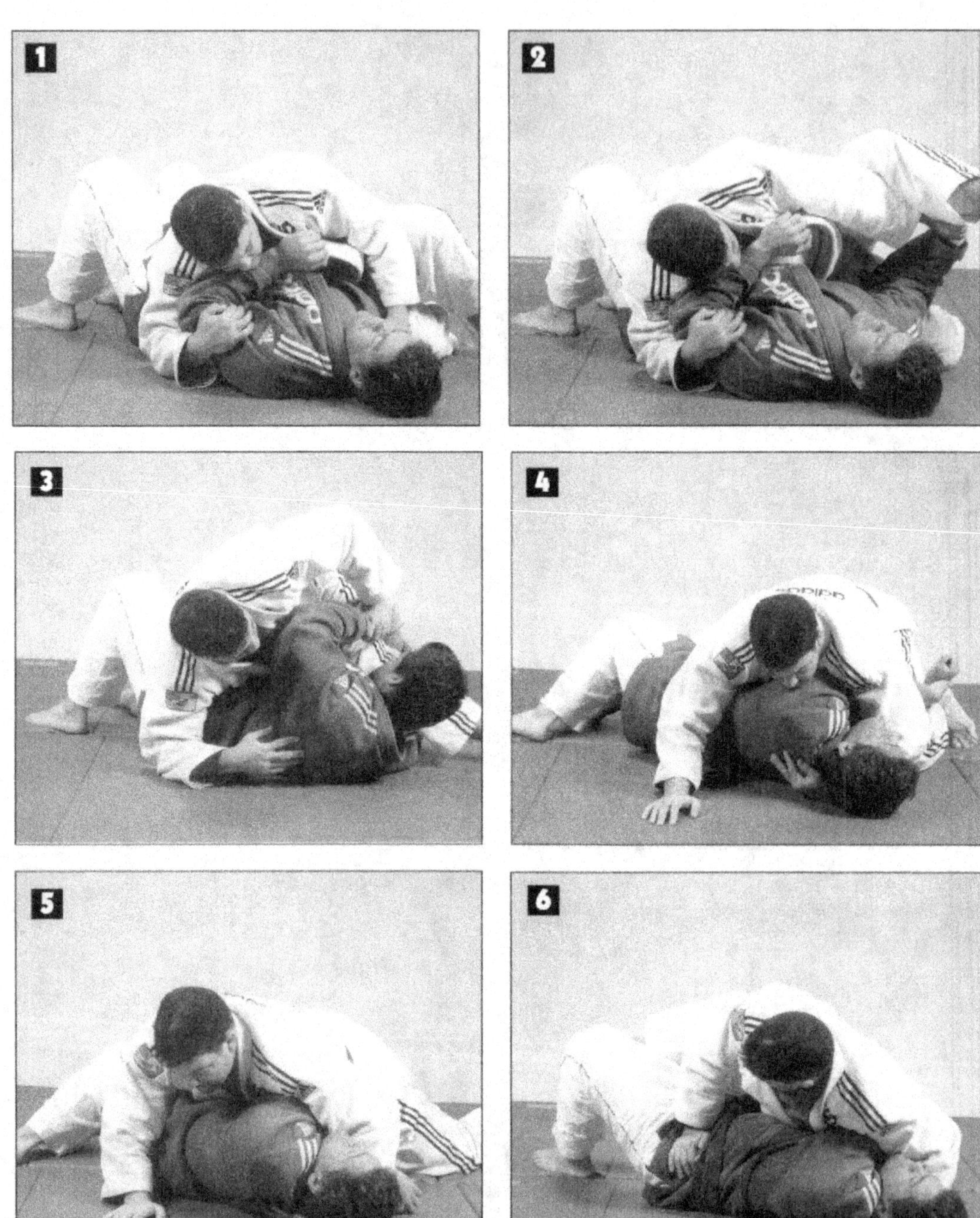

Side Control 52

Rigan controls the opponent from the side (1). He forces the opponent's right arm under his left leg (2), pulls the left arm with his left hand (3), and maintains control by applying pressure with his body (4). With both of the opponent's arms trapped, Rigan slides his hips to the right (5), and begins to push the opponent's right leg (6) with his right knee (7). To add pressure to the opponent's right hip, Rigan puts his right leg between the opponent's legs (8). Then he executes a finishing choke (9).

The opponent controls Rigan (1). Using both hands, Rigan pushes the opponent to the left and slides his hips to the right (2). This opens space for him to maneuver. Rigan starts to move his left leg around the opponent's right leg as he controls the opponent's right arm (3).

Side Control **53**

This helps him turn. Now facing the opponent (4), Rigan closes the guard (5).

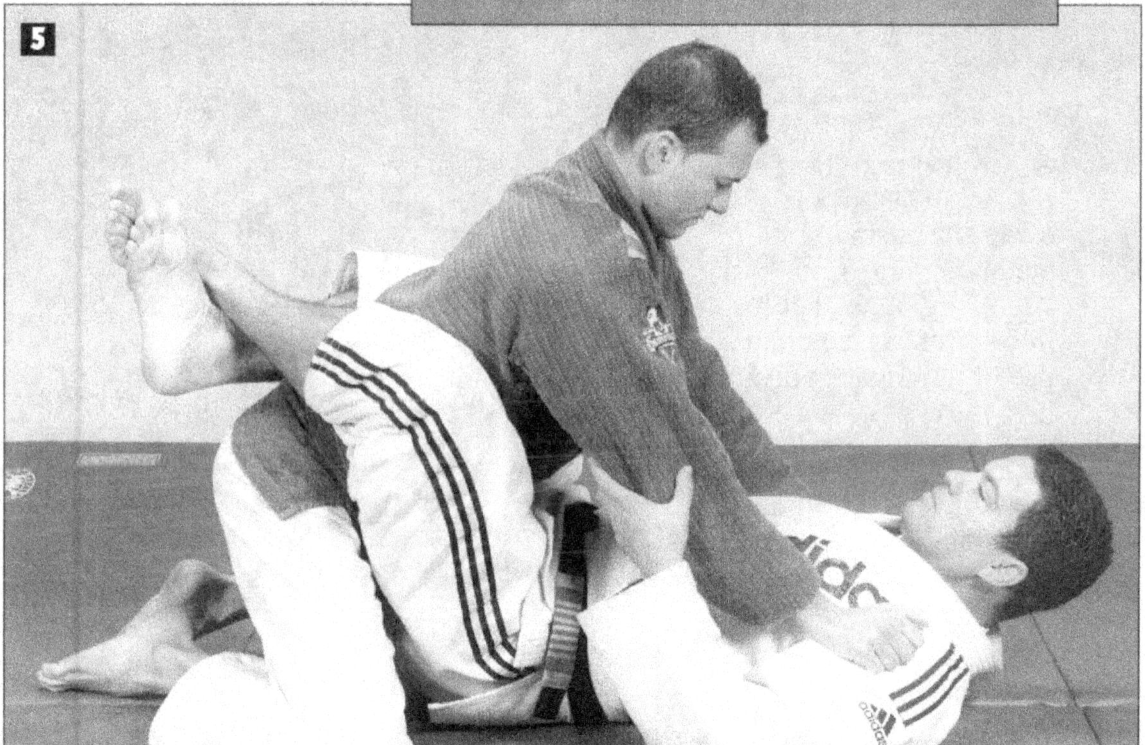

Controlled from the side (1), Rigan begins his escape by pushing his opponent away from him and swinging his left leg in front of the opponent's head (2-4). This enables him to adopt a new position and put his opponent inside his guard (5).

Side Control 54

In this movement, use your left arm to get momentum and balance yourself, as you simultaneously control the opponent's right arm, preventing him from stopping your movement.

The opponent controls Rigan from
the side (1). Notice that Rigan
prepares to create space by pushing
his opponent. Rigan rolls to the
right (2), keeping the action close
to the opponent's body (3). Rigan
quickly turns, grabs the opponent's
right hand (4), and pushes it back,

Side Control 55

nullifying the opponent's action (5). Rigan slides his left leg forward (6), and brings his opponent into the closed guard (7).

Rigan's opponent controls him
from the side (1). Notice that
his arm is under Rigan's neck.
Rigan traps the arm with his
head and locks his hands to
secure the opponent's right
arm (2). Rigan turns to the
right (3), maintaining the tight
grip on the opponent's arm (4),
until he is kneeling (5).

Side Control **56**

Rigan moves to the left, forcing the opponent to roll (6). The opponent is now in a vulnerable position (7) so Rigan can adopt the side control to initiate the offensive (8).

Rigan tries to control his opponent, who has established side
position (1). As soon as the opponent moves his right arm to control Rigan's head (2), Rigan grabs
the opponent's arm and belt (3).
Keeping a tight grip on both (4),
Rigan utilizes his hips, pulls hard
to the side (5), and throws him

Side Control **57**

to the other side (6).
Rigan can then adopt
side control to initiate an
attack (7).

This time the opponent assumes side control without putting his arm under Rigan's neck (1). This makes it impossible for Rigan to execute the previous escape. Instead, Rigan grabs the belt with both hands (2), and pulls hard, sending the opponent to the other side (3-4).

Side Control 58

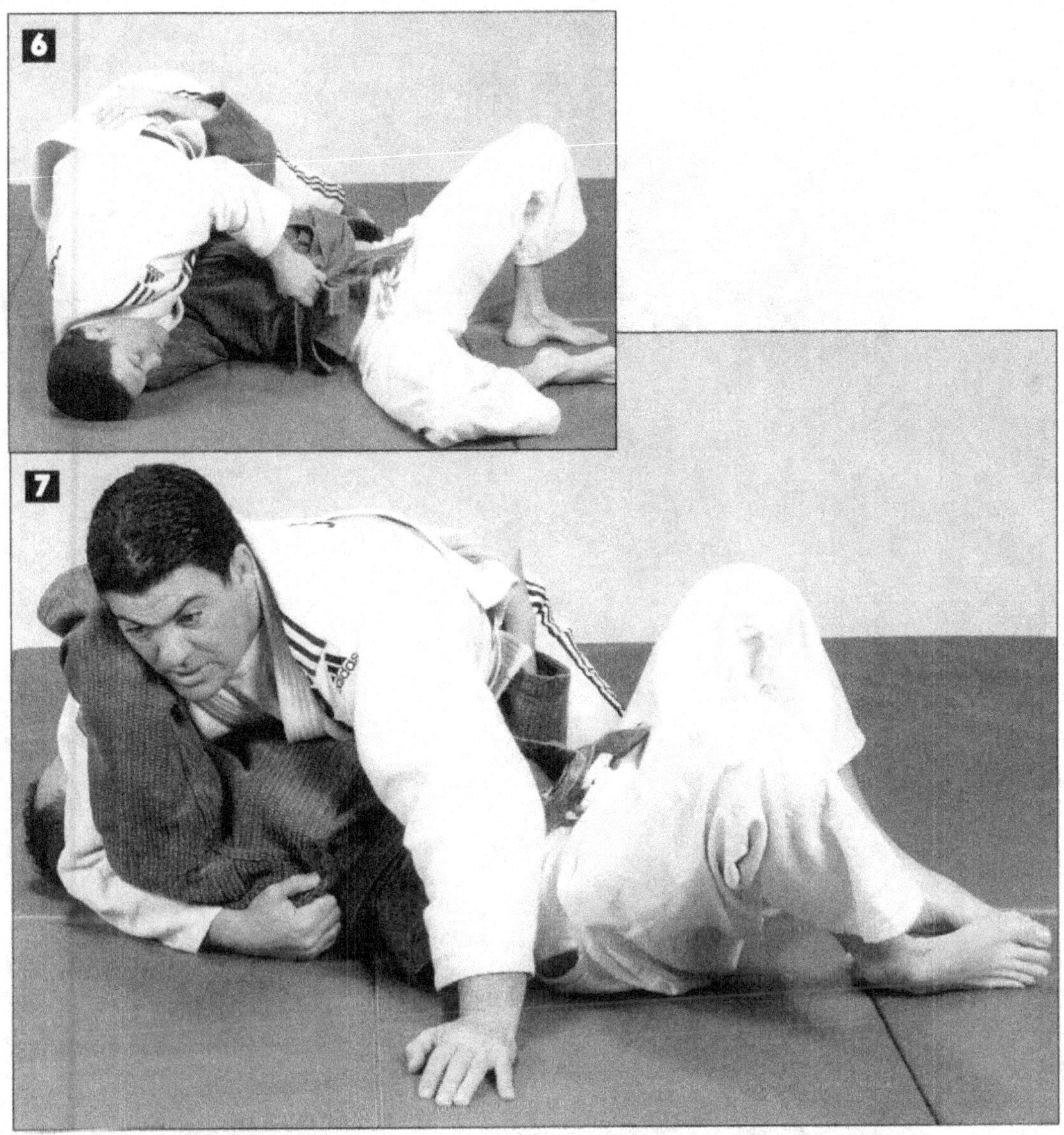

Rigan maintains tight control until the opponent lands (5). Immediately,
Rigan rolls (6) so he can assume side control and initiate the offensive (7).

The opponent controls Rigan (1). To gather momentum, Rigan lifts his legs
(2), and pushes the opponent away with both hands (3). The opponent ends
up flat on his back (4-5), and this enables Rigan to assume side control

Side Control 59

and begin the coun-
terattack (6).

The opponent tries to pass the guard from the side (1). Rigan reacts by grabbing the opponent's left arm and pushing it up (2). As Rigan does this, he raises his hips (3). This creates space and leverage to (4) throw the opponent over his body (5),

Side Control 60

6

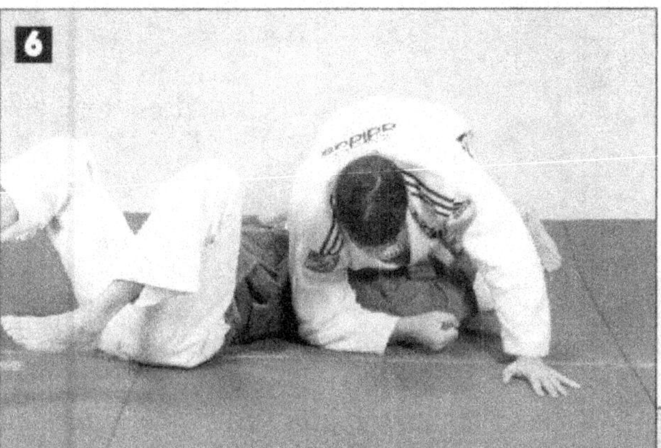

and onto the ground (6). Rigan can now apply full side control (7).

7

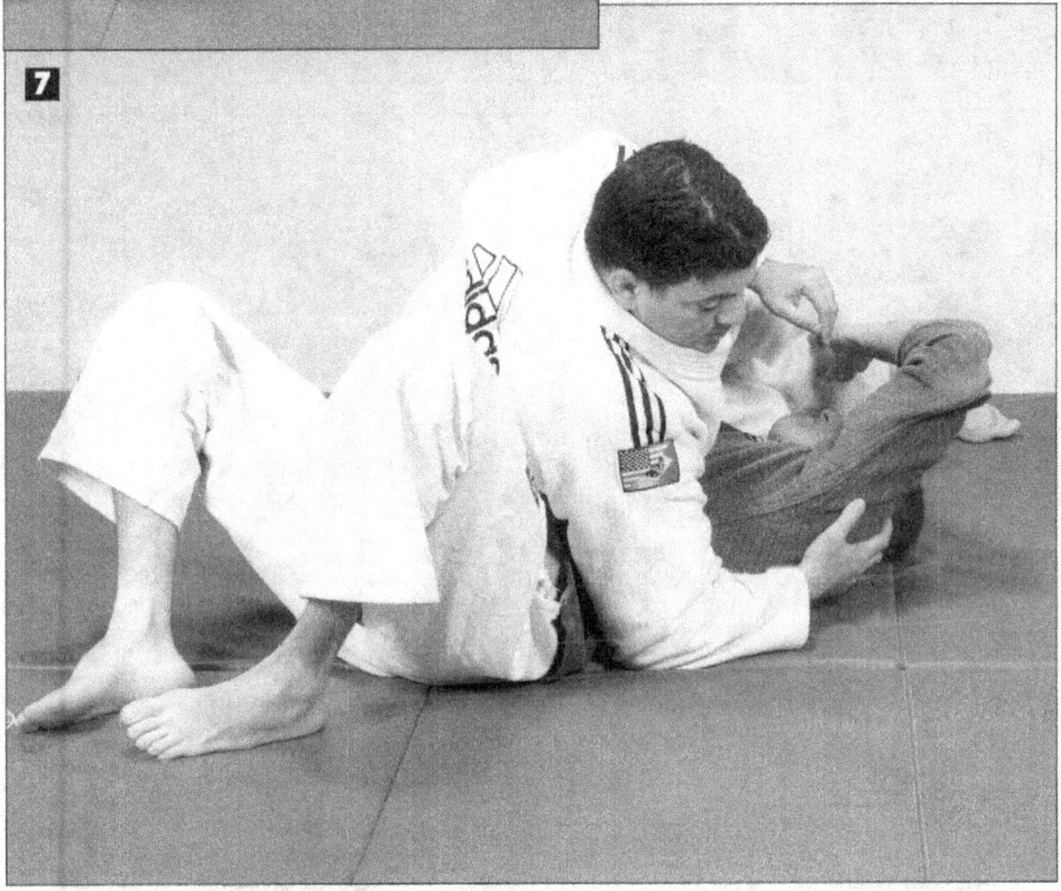

Rigan's opponent tries to initiate the offensive from the side (1). Using both hands, Rigan pulls the opponent's left arm, which unbalances him (2). Rigan slides his hips away from the opponent (3), so he can start lifting his right leg over him (4-5).

Side Control 61

Rigan starts moving to the back (6), where he can control the opponent more comfortably (7).

The opponent controls Rigan (1). Sliding his hips away, Rigan creates some space for himself (2-3) so he can move his legs out (4). He quickly moves into a kneeling position and grabs the opponent's thighs (5).

Side Control **62**

By pushing to the opposite side of the raised leg (6), Rigan forces the opponent to the ground (7), and immediately controls him from the side (8).

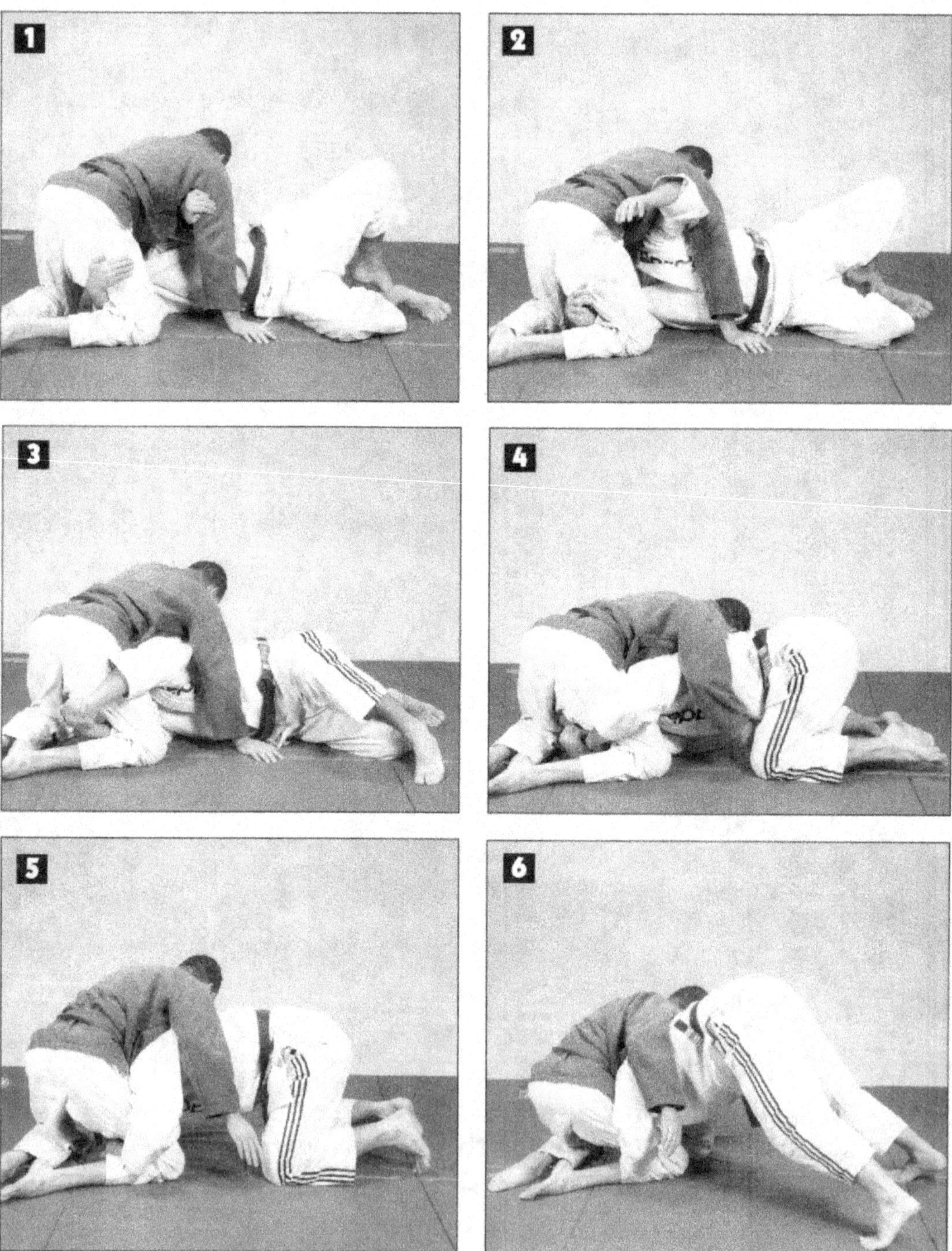

Side Control 63

The opponent establishes control from the side, but Rigan manages to slide back and insert his right hand between the opponent's legs and his left hand under the right armpit (1). Using these two points to establish momentum (2), Rigan begins to turn his body (3) until he's kneeling (4-5). He applies pressure with his body (6), creates space to bring his head out (7-8), and initiates the counterattack from the back (9).

Rigan's opponent establishes control from the side (1). With a tight grip on the opponent's collar and belt, Rigan pushes up (2-3), and rolls him to the right (4-5).

Side Control 64

Rigan moves his left leg outside the opponent's (6), mounts him to establish better control and prepares to initiate the counterattack (7).

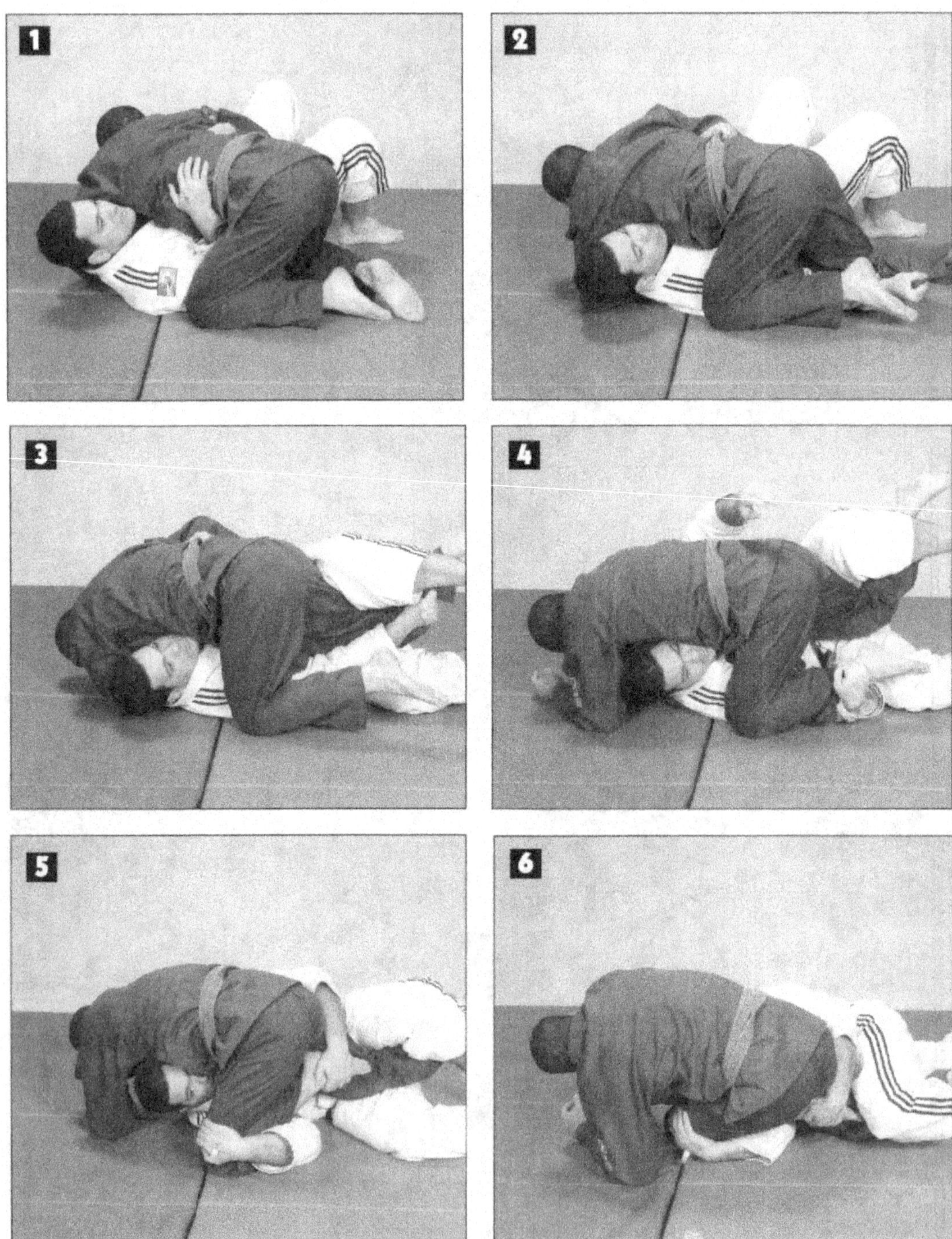

Side Control 65

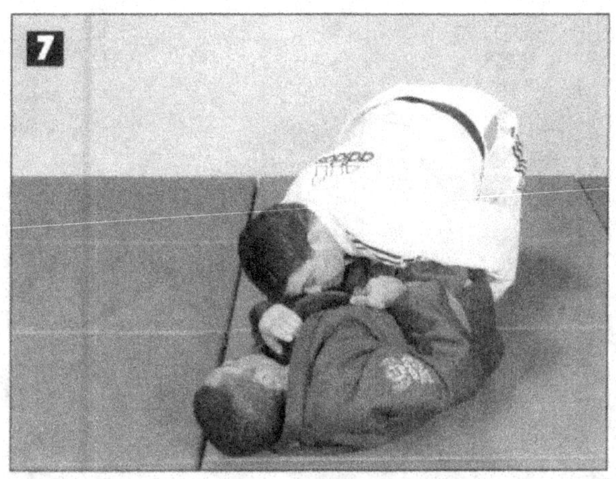

The opponent controls Rigan from the side (1). Rigan passes has right arm between the opponent's legs and grabs the adversary's pants (2). Rigan raises the opponent's leg so he can hook it with his left leg (3).

Rigan releases the opponent's right leg and immediately grabs the left ankle (4). He passes the ankle to his left hand as he grabs the opponent's left knee (5). This unbalances the opponent (6), rolling him over (7). Rigan can now initiate the final attack (8).

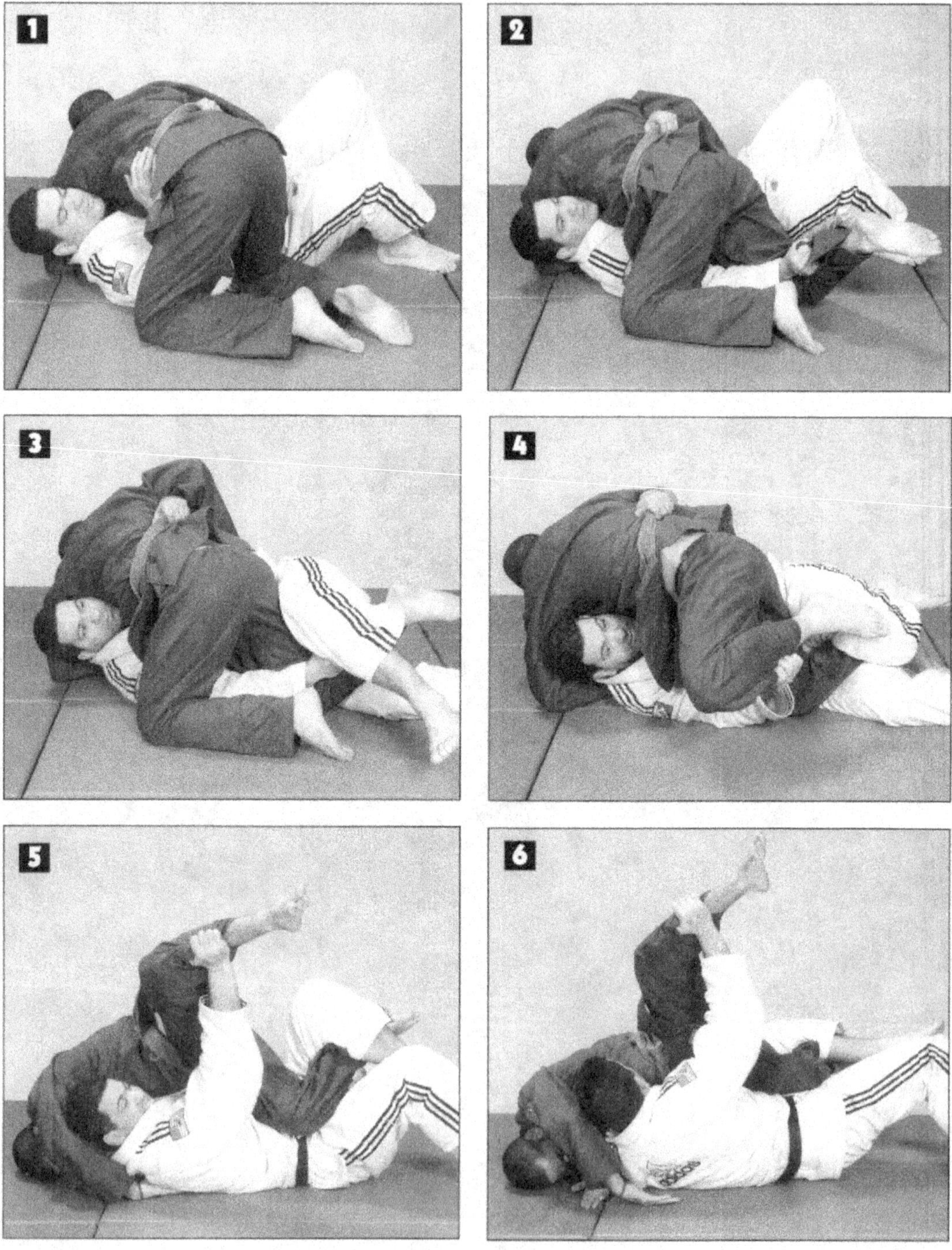

Side Control 66

The opponent controls Rigan from the side (1). Using his right hand, Rigan grabs the opponent's right leg (2). Notice how he reached between the adversary's legs. Rigan then pulls the leg up so he can hook it with his left leg (3). Rigan immediately switches grips and clamps onto the opponent's left leg (4). Rigan pushes hard to the left (5), throwing the opponent to the side (6-7). Rigan scrambles up (8), and initiates the offensive from the front (9).

The opponent controls Rigan
from the side (1). Rigan slides
his hips forward (2), and brings
his left arm out (3) so both
arms are on the opponent. He
pushes upward with his hips
(4), turns to the side (5),

Side Control **67**

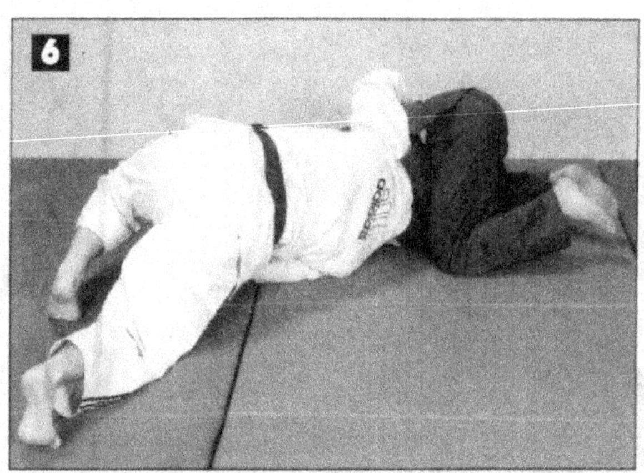

and escapes from the bottom (6). This enables him to go for full control from a more advantageous position (7).

The opponent controls Rigan from the side (1). Rigan slides his hips forward, extricates his left arm (2), and pushes upward with his hips (3). This time he turns the opposite Jiu-Jitsu way (4). This move enables him to escape from the

Side Control **68**

bottom (5). He goes for a
counterattack from the
back (6).

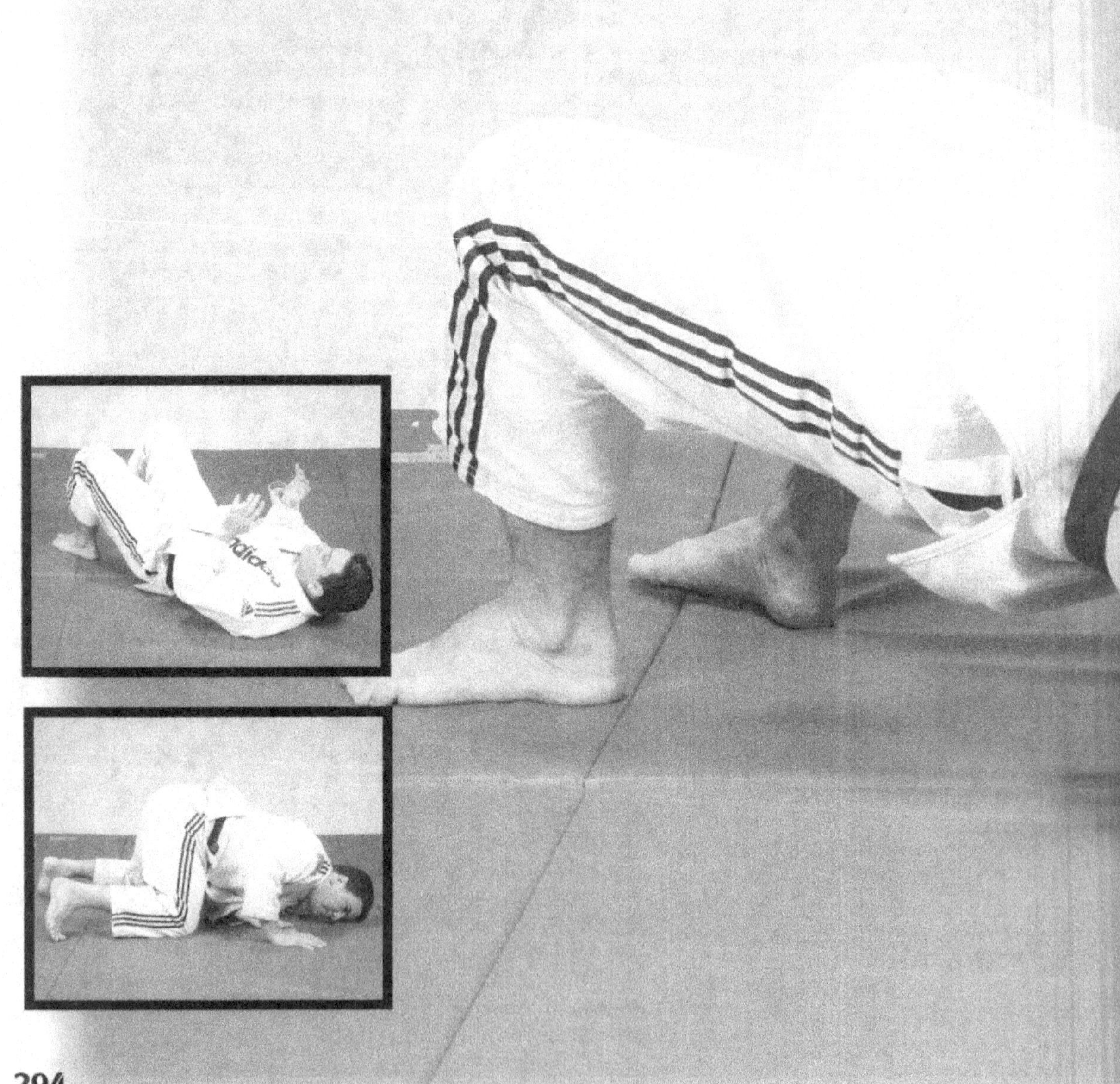

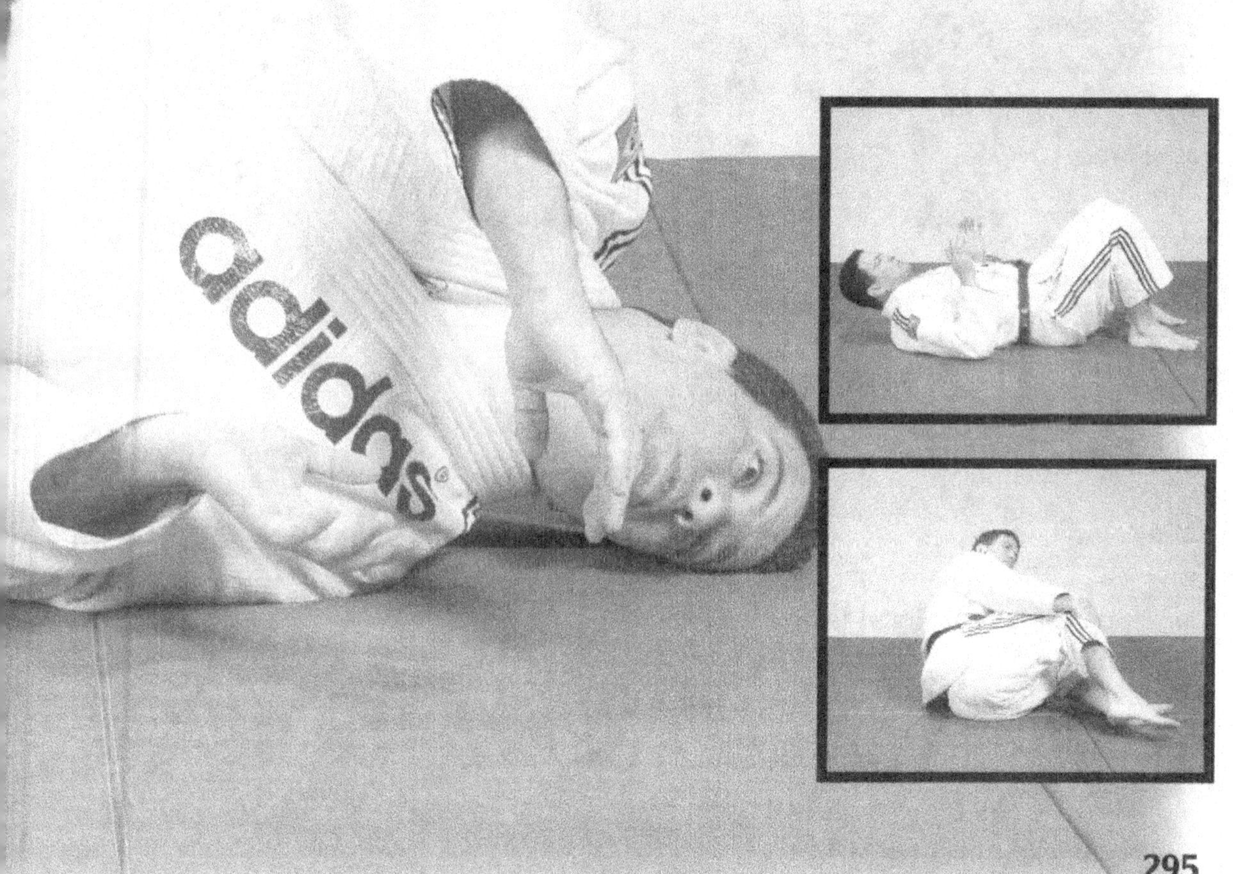

SIDE CONTROL DRILLS

VOL. 2

To fine-tune your body mechanics so you can escape from an opponent who has established side control, this is one of the most important drills you can do. To begin, Rigan is on his back with his knees up (1). While relaxing his left leg and right hip, Rigan moves his body weight to his left shoulder and right leg (2).

Side Control Drills **1**

He slides his hips back and simulates pushing with both arms (3). He ends up in the original position (4). Repeat the same movement on the other side (5-7). When sliding your hips back, it is important to have only two supporting points (left shoulder/right foot or right shoulder/left foot).

Rigan starts with his back on the ground (1). He pushes his hips upward (2) as he turns to the side and puts the weight on his left shoulder (3). Using his right leg for stability, he relaxes his left leg, turns to his left (4) and rolls into a kneeling position (5-6).

Side Control Drills 2

Do the drill for both sides. This is an excellent
drill to practice escaping from side control and
the mount.

Rigan starts on his back (1). He raises his legs (2), rolls over his left shoulder (3-4), and assumes the kneeling position (5). Do the drill for both sides.

Side Control Drills 3

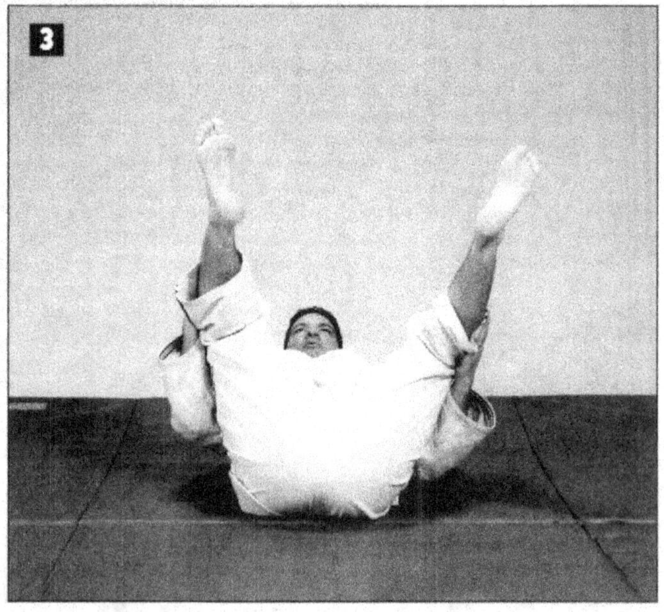

Rigan begins by sitting (1). He leans to the left (2), and allows his body to roll laterally (3) until he reaches the right side (4).

Side Control Drills 4

He's back in the original position and can now execute the drill to the other side (5).

Rigan starts in the bridge (1). Keeping his head in place, he starts circling to the right (2-3). During this movement, he maintains total control and balance. He moves his legs 180 degrees until he reaches the front position (4).

Side Control Drills 5

He repeats the movement to the other side (5-6) until he reaches the original position (7).

306

RULES
PART 2

Rules

**International Brazilian Jiu-Jitsu Federation
Technical Department of Regulations and Rules
Part 2**

A) Takedowns

A competitor scores two points if he knocks his opponent down, including from the back. If the athlete is thrown to the ground and does not land on his back, the opponent must pin him to the ground in the same position for at least three seconds to get the two points.

Note 1

A takedown is valid even if the competitor lands outside the fighting area if the athlete who performed the takedown had both feet in the fighting area while executing the technique.

Note 2

If an athlete has one of his knees on the ground and is taken down, his opponent will receive two points, provided that he had both feet on the ground. If the athlete has both knees on the ground and is knocked down, the competitor who performed the takedown will have to pass to the side and maintain this position to receive an advantage.

Note 3

When an athlete attempts a double-leg takedown while his opponent sits on the floor and executes a sweep, the athlete who attempted the takedown will not receive points. However, the one who executed the sweep will.

Note 4

When a competitor throws his opponent and ends up on the bottom, he will receive two points and the opponent (the one who was thrown) on top will receive the advantage. If the competitor executing the throw lands in his opponent's guard and is swept, both will receive two points.

B) Passing the Guard

A competitor will score three points when he is above his adversary or between his legs, moves to his opponent's side, establishes a perpendicular or longitudinal position over his adversary's trunk, dominates him and leaves him no space to move or to escape the position — even if he is on his side, back or facing down. This is passing the guard. Note: If the athlete that is underneath avoids the move by getting to his knees or standing, his opponent will not receive three points. Instead, he will be awarded an advantage.

C) Knee on the Belly

It's worth two points when the athlete on top puts his knee on his adversary's stomach and holds the opponent's collar or sleeve and belt.

Note: If the athlete on the bottom does not allow his adversary to put his knee onto his belly and if the competitor on top does not establish position completely, there will be no points awarded. Instead, it will be an advantage for the aggressor.

D) The Mount

A mount is worth four points and occurs when an athlete sits on his opponent's torso. The competitor being mounted can be on his stomach, side or back. The competitor who mounts his opponent can be on top of one of his opponent's arms but not both. It will also be considered a mount if the competitor has one knee and one foot on the ground.

Note: A competitor who is attempting a mount will not receive any points if his feet or knees are on his opponent's leg. If an athlete executes a triangle choke while in the guard and ends up mounting his opponent, it will be considered a sweep — not a mount. (See the section on the guard).

E) The Back Grab

A back grab nets four points. This occurs when an athlete grabs the adversary's back, holds his neck and wraps his own legs around the opponent's waist. The competitor executing the technique keeps his heels on the opponent's inner thighs, preventing him from moving. Note that the points will not be awarded if both heels are not properly positioned on the inner part of the adversary's thighs.

F) The Sweep

A sweep is worth two points. This occurs when the athlete on the bottom has his opponent in his guard (between his legs) or the half-guard (one of his adversary's legs is between his) and is able to get on top of his adversary by inverting his position.

Note 1

It will not be considered a sweep if the move does not begin from inside the guard or the half-guard.

Note 2

When the athlete executing a sweep advances his position to the back of his opponent, he earns two points.

Note 3

If a competitor who is in his opponent's guard attempts a sweep and both athletes return to their feet and the competitor attempting the sweep executes a takedown and stays on top, he will be awarded two points.

NEGATIVE POINTS (PENALTIES)

Following a third offense, a competitor can receive a penalty for avoiding engagement, stalling or not seeking ways to finalize the fight. As soon as the referee perceives that a competitor is stalling, he will begin a 30-second countdown and simultaneously warn the athlete. At the end of the 30 seconds, the referee will restart the fight and have the fighters stand. The offending athlete will be penalized two points.

5) Advantages

It is considered an advantage when an athlete attempts but does not complete any of the fundamental moves of the fight, such as a sweep, takedown, submission, etc.

- If one of the athletes attempts a technique, it is up to the referee to decide if he will award an advantage.
- While standing, if one of the competitors attempts a technique with aggressiveness and initiative, such as attempting a takedown or other finalizing move, he will receive an advantage.
- If the athlete attempts a technique and puts his adversary on the defensive during ground fighting, he will receive an advantage.
- If a competitor attempts a takedown and forces his opponent to lose his balance (even if the technique isn't completed), he will receive an advantage. A visible loss of balance during an attempted throw will also result in an advantage.
- During the closed guard (when the athlete on the bottom has his legs wrapped around his opponent's waist), it's possible to gain an advantage. Following are the circumstances in which a competitor can do that:

a) The athlete on top will earn the advantage by being on the offensive, trying to dominate his adversary's guard (pass the guard). For the referee to consider it an advantage, the athlete on top must come close to passing the guard, forcing his adversary to exert energy to regain position (half-guard, almost immobilizing, etc.)

b) The one underneath will earn the advantage if he almost sweeps his opponent, putting him in a dangerous position. He will also earn an advantage when he attempts a lock that forces his opponent to defend. Note: For the sweep attempt to be considered worthy of an advantage, the athlete underneath must open his legs.

c) If a competitor is attempting to pass the guard and unsuccessfully tries a foot lock while the adversary sits up, the competitor on top will receive an advantage point. In addition, if the competitor attempting the submission puts the opponent in visible danger, he will receive an advantage point.

continued in Volume 3

Epilogue

Now that you have finished this book, what have you learned? Hopefully nothing less than a series of practical and efficient techniques for becoming a successful Brazilian Jiu-Jitsu practitioner. These methods and training practices will help you succeed in competition and also to learn and grow after each defeat. These techniques have been developed by world-class competitors who have successfully applied them in elite competition. By using these same methods, you can also enjoy success in your own matches, even if you're not a world-class competitor. But simply reading through these pages is not enough. You must consistently practice each technique with a training partner, exploring all the possibilities of each position, until you obtain the desired results based on your body style, athletic ability, and physical attributes. Not all positions and techniques will work for every practitioner. Once you have a basic framework in place, you must fine-tune each position until it fits your game. The enjoyable part of Brazilian Jiu-Jitsu is that everyone can adapt and personalize it. While the basics are the same, the application of the basics is as different and varied as each practitioner. When practiced under the guidance of a qualified instructor, or with the assistance of a willing training partner, the principles and methods explained in these volumes will be effective. This is because they have been tested and proven for decades in the laboratory of practical experience and the crucible of real competition. Your task now is simply to go out and have fun with them!

— The authors